JACKSON KING

and the Morpher's heart

debbie hood

The Book Guild Ltd

First published in Great Britain in 2017 by
The Book Guild Ltd
9 Priory Business Park
Wistow Road, Kibworth
Leicestershire, LE8 0RX
Freephone: 0800 999 2982
www.bookguild.co.uk
Email: info@bookguild.co.uk
Twitter: @bookguild

Typeset in Minion Pro

Printed and bound in the UK by TJ International, Padstow, Cornwall

ISBN 978 1911320 388

British Library Cataloguing in Publication Data.
A catalogue record for this book is available from the British Library.

For Richard (Midge)
For making all the changes in my life good ones

With thanks to
Jak – For always being there to help
Mum (Pat) – For reading it first
Jo and Jackie – For reading it again
Kim – For her eyes

1.

The Beginning

The room was white, the ceiling, floor and walls, all white. Most of the things in the room were white as well, the bed, the machines, even the slightly buckled blind at the small window. The only non-white things were the dark red leather chair and the pale green blanket laid across the end of the bed.

From his position lying on the bed, Jack could see out the window. The room was on the third floor so he could only see the sky, which was swirling with dark grey clouds that had that slightly yellowish look they often have when a storm is on the way; England in August was known for its unpredictable weather. Shifting his gaze to the chair, Jack caught his grandma's eyes, she smiled at him, a small watery smile that made her face look even sadder, he tried to smile back but only managed a slight grimace. Jack wished he could reassure her that everything was going to be fine – better than fine in fact – that everything was going to be great from now on, but he was no longer feeling any of the confidence he had been feeling for the last few days, weeks and even months. Now that the moment was nearly here he only felt scared. He had always known this day would come, but he had always thought he would be better prepared for it when it arrived. He wished he could spare his grandma the anxiety he knew she would feel for the next few hours; it would be easier for him, he would be asleep.

***

Jack had been raised by his grandparents. Jackson Alan King had been born on the 11th February 1992. It had been a very cold night when Jack had arrived in the world. Born the only child of Sharon Anne King, father undisclosed by Sharon, Jack had been named Jackson, because Sharon said she liked the name, and Alan, after this grandfather. Jack's grandparents, Pam (a short, thin, kind woman who was a great cook and loved to fuss) and Alan (a tall, once powerfully built man who still looked imposing, but was just a big softie), had willingly taken over the task of raising him as soon as he came home from the hospital; when Sharon had announced that, as far as she was concerned, she had done her bit! Not that she did not love Jack, she did, it was just that Sharon was only eighteen. Having Jack had not been her plan; encouraged by her parents, she had kept the baby, but she was not ready to give up the social life she had worked hard to build for herself. Just seven months after Jack was born, Sharon was killed in a motorbike accident, not that Sharon had a motorbike, her parents would never have allowed her to own one as they had both witnessed what could happen to people when they came off motorbikes, but she had been on the back of her friend Mick's bike. They had taken a corner too fast and the road had been wet, Mick lost control of the bike and they had collided with an oncoming car. Sharon had been killed instantly, Mick died two days later in hospital and the driver of the car had walked away with a cut eye and a broken arm. Pam and Alan had been devastated; Jack could not remember his mother at all.

Pam and Alan made wonderful parents. They adored Jack,

and they gave him everything they could. They were both retired: Alan had been a policeman and Pam a nurse, they had met through work when Alan had been brought into casualty one night after being attacked by a burglar he had disturbed and Pam had been the nurse in charge. It had been love at first sight, she had cleaned and bandaged his wounds and he had asked her to dinner. Sharon had been their only child; with her gone, they lavished all their love on their grandson.

They lived in a four bedroom detached house in a small Sussex village called Ashfield that bordered the Ashdown Forest. They had bought the house when Pam had discovered she was pregnant with Sharon. Thinking at that time that they would have at least three children, they had bought the biggest house they could afford, once they realised they would only ever be blessed with one child, they were already happy and settled in their home and did not ever consider moving somewhere smaller.

As a baby, Jack slept a lot, he rarely cried, he just ate and slept; this made him a very easy baby to raise and, although Pam and Alan were grateful that they did not have many sleepless nights, it did make Pam wonder. Having raised her own child, she knew that even the best of babies often had bad days. Not Jack, though, he was the perfect baby. When Jack reached the age when he started to learn to walk, however, Pam and Alan realised something was wrong. Jack had no energy, unlike most children who never seem to need any sleep, Jack still needed a lot of rest. He was quite skinny and pale, and was always getting colds and other minor illnesses. At the age of three, the doctors, following numerous tests, announced that Jack had a problem with his heart, which would deteriorate over time. Pam and Alan were once again devastated, fearing they would lose their precious boy. The doctors assured them that the condition was treatable with drugs, but that eventually a heart transplant would be necessary to allow Jack to lead a normal life.

Growing up, Jack found at an early age that he preferred animals to people. Being shy, pale, skinny, and wanting to sleep all the time, Jack found it hard to make friends. He found that animals did not judge you, they did not care what you looked like or how good you were at sports, they did not even care if you smelled bad; as long as you were nice to them they tended to be nice back. Jack found that most animals he came across seemed to take to him, whether it was because he came across as gentle or did not make sudden moves, Jack did not know, but he was often being told the same thing if he stopped to pat a dog in the street. The owners would say, 'He doesn't usually like strangers, but he seems to like you.'

Jack's favourite place to go on outings was the zoo, any zoo. He loved to see all the animals and, although he would have preferred to see them in their natural habitat rather than in cages, there was still something magical about the zoo for him. Again all the animals seemed to like him; they turned his way when he approached and those that were accessible to the public (mainly the smaller animals in the petting zoo) always headed straight for him. The larger animals, even the big cats, watched him with a calm interest as if they knew he was a friend.

As a family they had never had pets; Pam was very house proud and, although she liked animals, she had no desire to share her house with them. Despite his constant asking and whining, Pam would not give in and let Jack have the dog he so wanted, or even a hamster. One day in the school summer holidays when Jack was twelve, he was sitting in the garden reading a book when a tiny cat came over the fence. Jack had been fascinated watching the cat, trying to keep as still as possible so as not to frighten it away. It was a very pale tabby colour with strange bluish-green eyes that seemed to stare right at him. The cat had walked casually around the garden, sniffing at plants and watching insects buzzing from flower to flower. Although it stared at him, it did not come too close and would not approach him when he held out his hand and rubbed the tips of his fingers together in a welcoming gesture. It stayed about ten minutes and then jumped lightly back over the fence from where it had come. As soon as the cat was out of sight, Jack jumped up and ran over to the fence and looked over it to see where it was, but the cat had gone. All Jack could see was a quiet road with a car pulling away from the curb. Disappointed, he returned to his book. The following day Jack was once again in the garden, reading, when the tiny cat appeared again. It did the same as the day before: came over the fence, sniffed around the garden, held Jack in its unusual bluish-green stare that seemed almost human and then disappeared again. This same pattern repeated itself for the next few days, always the same: the cat would come in, sniff around, stare at him and then leave. On the sixth day, however, the cat approached Jack, purring, and let Jack stroke it. They became firm friends. The cat wore no identification, but Jack decided it was a girl and, not knowing what her real name was, named her Poppy, because she liked to smell the flowers. Every day she visited him in the garden, Jack was worried that when he returned to school she would stop coming to see him, but she seemed to sense there was a change and she started visiting him after school. He had asked his gran on several occasions if they could keep Poppy, but she always answered the same, 'She's not ours, Jack, she has an owner somewhere.'

'So why does she always come and see me then?' Jack would ask sulkily, but he knew she was right.

'Because she likes you,' Pam had said kindly, 'but if you try to keep her, you might drive her away. Cats are very independent animals, Jack, they come and go as they please.'

Pam had relented slightly and bought some cat food so Jack could feed Poppy, but Poppy would not touch the food. She would never eat or drink anything at Jack's house, even when he tried to tempt her with fresh fish or chicken, she would just look at him with her strange eyes and purr. She never stopped visiting though; every day from then on, come rain or shine, term time or holidays, Poppy and Jack spent time together and, even though strictly speaking she was not Jack's cat, he came to think of her as his.

Jack went to East Green School in the nearby town of Tenbridge, which was about three miles from Ashfield. Jack did not enjoy school, he found it hard to make friends and, due to his health problems, was unable to participate in any sports or physical activities, which excluded him from one of the best ways to get to know his fellow students: becoming part of team. Most of the other kids he went to school with simply ignored him. There was one boy, however, Eric Tarver, who did not ignore Jack, though Jack wished with all his heart that he would. Eric seemed to go out of his way to make life difficult and embarrassing for Jack. Jack would have found it hard to like Eric anyway, just for the fact that he was good at everything, both sports and academics and all the girls loved him because he was tall and good-looking, with black hair and blue eyes but Jack thought the eyes looked cold and unfriendly. Eric and his gang (consisting of three other boys: Matt Middleton, a small ferrety boy with mousey hair, a pointed nose and an unpleasant smell, Toby Ward, a fierce brute of a boy who made some of the teachers look small and Danny Cole, a small clever boy who was Eric's cousin), made it their job to make Jack's school life as unpleasant as possible. Jack never understood Eric's motivation for acting the way he did. There seemed no need for Eric to try to impress anyone by picking on the weak kid; he already had everyone's undivided attention wherever he went. Jack could only assume that, although it was not obvious to everyone, Eric had a very ugly mean streak. It started on the first day at secondary school. The first day Jack and Eric met, Eric had strolled into the first lesson, sat down and, upon spotting Jack, had immediately shouted across the classroom, 'Oi, skinny kid, what's wrong with you, you sick or something?' to which most of the class looked in Jack's direction, awaiting some sort of response and Matt, Toby and Danny had laughed cruelly.

Jack had felt the colour rise in his cheeks, he had no retort and nothing remotely clever or funny occurred to him. He simply sat in his chair getting redder and redder. After a few minutes most of the other kids had got bored, but not Eric. Sensing a sick sort of victory he carried it on, 'Oi, sick kid, I'm talking to you.'

Luckily for Jack, Mrs Neville, the strict maths teacher, had arrived at that moment and that had put a stop to it, but from then on, Eric had his target.

At the beginning of Jack's third term at secondary school, a new boy started. He was short and very slightly overweight, he had blond spiky hair and kind grey eyes that had a naughty twinkle. Their first lesson together, Mr Humphries, the geography teacher had sat them next to each other. Looking embarrassed the boy introduced himself.

'I'm Dennis Gribben,' he said, holding out his hand to Jack.

Jack took his hand and shook it saying, 'Hi. I'm Jack King.'

Dennis, sensing he was getting a good response carried on, 'We just moved here from Scotland. I'm not Scottish, by the way. Well, I am half Scottish: my mum's Scottish, but I haven't got the accent. We moved up there a few years ago when my gran got ill, so my mum could look after her, but she died so we moved back, which I'm glad about because it's a lot warmer down here. I'm not glad because my gran died, obviously. I've got an older sister, Sophie, haven't any pets, though, 'cos I'm allergic… you got any brothers or sisters or pets?'

'No,' said Jack, 'although, actually, I sort of have a cat'.

'How can you sort of have a cat?' asked Dennis. 'Either you have a cat or you don't.'

'Well it's not my cat, it belongs to someone else but spends a lot of time at my house,' and he explained all about Poppy.

'I'm allergic to cats,' Dennis grumbled.

'I don't have any brothers or sisters, though,' Jack added quickly, 'not even sort of ones.'

Dennis laughed, 'Lucky you,' he said thoughtfully, 'my sister's a pain.'

Dennis went on to explain that his dad was called Brian and was a builder and his mum was called Elaine and was a hairdresser. Dennis also explained about his allergies.

'I'm asthmatic,' he explained. 'And I'm allergic to lots of stuff too: pollen, penicillin, raspberries, well, loads of stuff really. It doesn't really bother me much, I'm used to it. So tell me about you.'

'Er, what do you want to know?' Jack asked slightly alarmed.

'Anything,' said Dennis. 'What you like, what you don't like, what's your favourite sport,' he suggested.

'I like animals,' Jack said thoughtfully. 'I don't much like school and I don't really have a favourite sport, although I do like to watch people running.'

'Why don't you like sport?' asked Dennis.

'Because I'm no good at it,' replied Jack.

'Why not?' Dennis persisted.

'Because I have a problem with my heart,' Jack offered quietly. 'I have to take drugs every day and one day I'll need a transplant.'

'Yikes,' Dennis breathed. 'That sucks, poor you.' Then he added, 'Ha, like me. I can't do sports either.'

They were both quiet for a while and then Dennis whispered, 'Does it hurt?'

'Does what hurt?' Jack asked, puzzled.

'You know, your heart thing.'

'Not most of the time, no,' Jack replied, smiling, 'The

drugs make me feel sick and I'm always tired, but I don't have much pain.'

'I get pain,' Dennis said. 'If I so much as see a long-haired cat I start sneezing and my eyes go red and I get all blotchy, then I start wheezing and have to use my inhaler. It's a nightmare.'

Jack smiled and they both went quiet again, but they were both realising they had a lot in common, neither of them could participate in anything physical and neither were any good at making friends. At that moment, Eric noticed the new boy.

'Oi, sick kid, who's your fat girlfriend?'

Jack did not look round, but Dennis looked to see who was talking and who they were talking to. Realisation dawning, he said, 'Oh great, here we go again'.

Jack smiled sadly, but he did not feel particularly sad, as he was no longer alone.

Having a friend was one of the best things that had ever happened to Jack. It was so nice to have someone to laugh with, share secrets with and even just do homework with. Having someone on his side made such a difference: when Eric and Matt took all of Jack's books and scattered them across the football field, Dennis was there to help him collect them and when Eric pushed Dennis over in the mud, Jack was there to pick him up.

Jack was not surprised that Eric and his gang would pick on anyone they could; they were totally indiscriminate in their discrimination. One day a new boy had turned up at school in the year below Jack. He walked with a limp due to the fact that he had a club foot. He was obviously aware that some people would find this funny and make a scene, and it seemed he was completely used to being treated the way Eric treated him. He had a strange sort of defence mechanism that made him 'ham it up' whenever Eric and his gang were about to start bullying him; if he was walking across the playground he would make the limp very noticeably pronounced, far worse than it really

was, making his hips sway out too far. This had the effect that
Eric would laugh and, although this did not stop the bullying
altogether, it seemed to ease it a bit. His lop-sided swagger had
earned him the nickname 'Stump'. Jack and Dennis had tried
to make friends with him, but he had shunned all their efforts
to know him.

'Sorry,' he had said, 'I've spent my life being bullied because
of the way I walk, I look at you guys and I see two fellow freaks
who have also suffered. Not being funny or anything, but I
have enough of my own problems, I don't need yours as well.'

Jack and Dennis had been surprised at this, remembering
they had both felt much better having each other to help them
through the bad times, but it was his choice. Stump did not
last long, he only stayed at the school six months before his
father was relocated.

Time at school carried on for Jack in the same vein for the
next couple of years. Dennis was a regular visitor at the King
house, staying weekends and joining in when Alan and Pam
took Jack on trips. The one thing that had surprised both the
boys was Dennis' reaction when he had first met Poppy. Having
never been able to go very near cats or dogs without sneezing
violently and coming out in an itchy rash, Dennis was not too
keen to be in close proximity to Poppy. On Dennis' first visit to
the King house, he and Jack had been in the lounge watching
TV when Poppy had appeared, meowing at the patio doors.
Jack had automatically got up to let her in when Dennis had
jumped out of his chair, shouting, 'Yikes, Jack, don't let it in
here,' and had started backing quickly out of the room.

'But it's Poppy,' Jack had said by way of an explanation. 'I
always let her in, she won't understand if I don't,' and he had
opened the door.

Poppy had walked slowly into the room and stared at the
now terrified looking Dennis, who was backed up against the
far wall.

'She won't hurt you,' Jack laughed.

'But I'm allergic,' explained Dennis, 'any minute now I'll start swelling up and sneezing.'

But Dennis had not started swelling up and sneezing. He just stood there staring at Poppy and she stood staring back at him. After a few minutes, Jack had said, 'Where's the swelling, Den?'

'Dunno,' Dennis had answered, puzzled. 'It's usually much quicker than this.'

So they had waited a bit more, Jack holding Poppy in his arms so she would not go too close to Dennis, but still nothing happened. Jack moved a bit closer to Dennis and still nothing happened, so he moved even closer, still nothing. Eventually Jack was standing right next to Dennis and still nothing happened.

'I don't understand,' said Dennis. 'I've never been this close to cat before and not at least sneezed,' he added.

'Well, she does have very short fur,' Jack offered. 'Maybe you're only allergic to long-haired cats?'

'Maybe,' Dennis agreed, unconvinced.

Despite the lack of any sort of reaction, Dennis would not touch Poppy, but agreed to her being in the room. No matter how many times after that Dennis visited the King house when Poppy was there, he never so much as sniffed.

The boys also hung out at Dennis' house. Dennis' parents loved Jack; they were so pleased to see their son finally enjoying school. One of the main points of interest for Jack at Dennis' house was Dennis' older sister Sophie and her friends. Being two years older than Jack and Dennis, Sophie and her twin friends, Livvie and Lucinda Madingly, at sixteen were the sophisticated older women and the boys learned a lot, listening at Sophie's closed bedroom door when she had sleepovers and the girls were discussing boys. Jack found the girls to be rather giggly and silly, but their point of view was so alien and interesting that it was compulsive listening. Of course the girls had no interest in the young geeky boys, finding them to be more a nuisance than anything else, but for Jack it was an eye-opener into the world of females. At fourteen, Jack had never really noticed girls before; most of the ones at school ignored him and he barely registered them when they had flocked around Eric and his gang. Being raised by his grandparents, Jack's only female company had been his grandma and she had been in her fifties when he had been born. He could not remember his mother and did not have any sisters, cousins or aunties. Suddenly Jack was noticing girls everywhere. Not that they noticed him. His teen years had been kind enough. He had suddenly shot up in height, although all this really did was make him look even skinnier. He had deep brown eyes, mid-brown hair and a pleasant face that had never had to suffer the embarrassment of acne, but he was still pale and sickly looking and no girl at school would look twice at him, especially when Eric was around. Dennis had no more luck with girls than Jack, being short, slightly overweight and a bit wheezy.

Just after Jack turned fifteen, he noticed a new girl at school he had never seen before. She was small and pretty with bluish-green eyes and long tawny blonde hair; she moved very gracefully, as if she was a dancer, and Jack found his eyes drawn to her whenever she was around. Dennis had never noticed her either, so they assumed she must be new. She appeared to be very popular with both the girls and the boys, especially Eric, which came as no surprise to Jack, as Eric always hung around with the pretty girls. A couple of days after they first noticed the girl, Dennis came half running, half walking into school shouting for Jack.

'What?' Jack had asked.

'The new girl,' Dennis had panted. 'Her name is Katherine Felix, she's just moved here from… oh I don't know, somewhere abroad. She's in our year and Eric has already asked her out. And get this, she said no!'

'How do you know all this?' Jack had asked.

'Soph,' Dennis answered. 'I overheard her telling one of her friends on the phone. Great, huh? I wish I'd seen Eric's face when she turned him down, bet that's a first.'

Jack had laughed along with Dennis, imagining how Eric would have reacted to not getting his way, but in the back of his head he was processing the information on Katherine and wondering if Eric was not her type, then who was?

A few days later, when Jack was crossing the playground to get to his next class, he noticed Katherine sitting alone on a bench by the edge of the field. It was hard to tell from a distance, but it looked as though she was crying. Even though Jack had never been able to just walk up to someone and start talking, he thought he should see if she was okay. He changed his course and headed towards the bench where she sat, he had only gone a few steps when Eric appeared from nowhere and started heading towards Katherine as well.

He spotted Jack, realised immediately what Jack's intensions were and shouted, 'Oi, sick kid, leave the poor girl alone. Looks like she's upset enough without having to catch something from you.'

Jack felt his face go red and he tripped over his own feet while quickly trying to change course back to the original direction he had been taking, wishing with all his heart that Eric would fall flat on his face in the mud. He would just love to see Eric get his comeuppance. Later on the same day in history, he had been sitting not far from Katherine. At one point, he had looked in her direction to see if she was still upset and could have sworn she had been looking at him, he had immediately looked back at his history book, knowing his face was going red and feeling something hot in his stomach. For the rest of the lesson he had been unable to concentrate on history, wanting only to take a peek at Katherine to see if she would look at him again. By the end of the lesson he had convinced himself that he had probably imagined it and that she had been looking at someone behind him. As he got up to leave he caught her eye and this time he was shocked to see she smiled at him; a small, shy smile, but a smile none the less. Completely forgetting how to move any of the muscles in his face, he just stared stupidly and she, getting embarrassed, had quickly walked away.

His teen years saw Jack's health deteriorate. The little energy he had was almost completely gone and he was taking a lot of time off school. This bothered him because he was missing Dennis and, although he would admit this to no one, not even Dennis, he was missing seeing Katherine. Since the first time she had smiled at him, (no girl had ever smiled at him before), he had gone out of his way to pass her in corridors and on the playground and she had not disappointed him, she gave him her small, but quite startling smile whenever she saw him. With her small red lips and even white teeth, she had a very pretty smile, very pretty indeed. Although she had first appeared popular when she had started at the school, she had in the weeks that followed shown herself to be something of a loner. Despite the numerous offers she'd had to sit with various different groups of people at lunchtime, she always chose to eat alone, looking deep in thought and a little sad. Jack also thought she spent a lot of time staring at him, smiling if he caught her eye and looking away, but she always seemed to be looking back at him when he chanced another look. Dennis had confirmed these suspicions by saying every time he looked at her he was pretty sure she was staring at Jack, though he had no better idea than Jack as to why she was staring.

It was at this time, when Jack was spending a lot of time at home that the dreams started. At first, Jack did not realise they were so similar, sometimes he did not even remember having them at all. After about the fifth or sixth dream, Jack started remembering them more and more clearly. They bothered him, not because they were frightening or upsetting, but because they kept recurring and that had to mean something. They were always similar, though slightly different. Jack would be running, running very fast; sometimes through fields, sometimes through a town, sometimes he dreamed he was running through snow and sometimes the sun was shining and the weather was warm. Jack thought he knew exactly why he dreamed about running, because it was the one thing he had never been able to do and the one thing he had always wanted to do. In the dreams he was always running away from something and towards something; sometimes he thought he could see the thing he was running to, but it was always too far away to see it properly. He thought he could guess what he was running from, most likely it was Eric and, at times, he also thought he had a good idea what he was running to, though he always got embarrassed so he tried not to think too much about that. More worrying, though, than the dreams, he also started to have waking dreams or hallucinations. These scared Jack enough that he kept them to himself, deciding that it was obviously an effect of the drugs and that, as soon as he had a new heart, they would stop. He decided there was really no need to worry anyone with them, even his doctor. After all hadn't the doctor warned him the drugs could cause side effects, not that he had been very specific with what the side effects might be, but Jack guessed they were probably different in everyone. The hallucinations, like the dreams, were always similar, though slightly different. The first time it had happened he had been alone in his room, he had been angry because he'd had a run-in with Eric. Jack had been walking home, having just got off the bus from school, minding his own business when Eric had jumped out from behind a tree and thrown wet mud at him. Luckily for Jack, Eric was a lousy shot and only a small amount of the mud had actually hit him on the shoulder, but it had made him very angry.

'Leave me alone!' he had shouted at Eric.

'Not a chance, sick boy,' Eric had replied, laughing, and with that he had run off.

Jack had gone straight to his room when he got home to change his clothes. As he took off his shirt to replace it with a t-shirt, he felt a very sharp pain in his hand and, looking down, could have sworn the index finger on his right hand looked quite a lot shorter than all the others, about half the length it usually was. Looking at it properly, it was obviously fine, but it had been weird. His eyes or, because of the pain, more likely his mind, was playing tricks on him. After that every so often he would, just for the briefest of moments, feel actual pain and think he saw some part of his body looking not quite right, but as soon as he looked properly, it would of course be perfectly normal. It was the pain that seemed the most real; he could feel physical pain even though he knew it was not real. Each time he had one these hallucinations, he felt hot and clammy and his breath got faster, his heartbeat increased and he had what he could only assume was a mild panic attack. This feeling only lasted a very short time and it was an involuntary reaction. Jack knew he was imagining these things and therefore there was no reason to be afraid, but he just could not stop his body panicking.

The drugs he was taking, although causing the dreams and hallucinations to become more frequent, were no longer performing as well as they had on Jack's heart and the doctors were getting more concerned that the time for a transplant was rapidly approaching. Obviously the problem was going to be finding a donor; Jack had been on the register for many

years, but the urgency had never been
few months Jack was unable to do anythin
sleep. He could not go to school, so Den
as he could, keeping Jack up-to-date with
gossip. The one thing Jack was most intereste
about Katherine. He had been thinking abou ⸻ while
he had some time on his hands. He was confused about why
she kept smiling at him, he did not know why she smiled,
but he liked the fact that she did. Dennis did not fail him, he
came armed with news that Eric was still pestering Katherine,
following her everywhere she went, asking her out, and
Katherine was still turning him down and keeping herself to
herself.

Apart from the love and support Jack got from his
grandparents and Dennis, the one thing that kept him going
was Poppy: she came every day and even sat on his bed when
he was too weak to get up. She would lay still, purring, while
he stroked her soft fur and he found this simple action and her
contented sounds calmed his troubled mind. She still refused
food and water from Jack and never stayed late in the evening,
preferring to get home and maybe avoid being shut out for
the night or maybe she liked being out all night prowling the
streets, Jack could not know, but he always hated it when she
left, wishing she would just choose to stay and live with him.

Then one day, out of the blue, the call came: there was a heart.
A middle-aged but very fit man had been crossing the road
and had been hit by a lorry. The blood and tissue types were a
match, Jack needed to get to the hospital. Jack had been sleeping
at the time of the call; Pam had come and woken him up. It had
been a panic. Even though Jack and his grandparents had been
waiting for the call, even though Jack had had his bag packed
for several weeks and even though it was what they had been
praying for, it was still a shock and panic had ensued. There had

no conversation during the journey to the hospital; each of them had been lost in their own thoughts. Jack's thoughts had been mainly wondering about how much pain there would be. He was also concerned that his grandparents were not young anymore and they did not need this sort of stress. The one thing he tried hard not to think about was the possibility that he might not survive the next few hours. When they had arrived at the hospital, Alan had dropped them at the entrance while he went to park the car. Jack and Pam had walked hand in hand through the door, Jack had been ushered into a wheelchair and they had been rushed through the building and into the lift. They had filled out some paperwork, though Jack had no idea what is was, he just went into autopilot while he undressed, all the time maintaining the stony silence.

***

So here he was, lying on the white bed in the white room with his grandma sitting on the red leather chair and his granddad parking the car. This was not how Jack had expected to feel. He had thought he would feel relieved, even excited, at the prospect of a new heart. He had not expected to feel scared. Even the pre-med had only taken a slight edge off his fear, though it had helped to calm his raging and scarily weak heart. His mouth was dry, his hands were shaking and he wished it was all over. Dr Noah had been through the details a hundred times with all three of them, they knew exactly what was going to happen and how long everything was likely to take. They had been warned there was always a risk with any operation but Dr Noah had performed this procedure many times before, Jack would be in safe hands.

The door opened and a pretty young woman put her head in the room, she smiled, 'Won't be long now, Jack. Are you feeling okay?'

Jack nodded, unable to speak.

Pam looked back at Jack, 'Don't worry, sweetie,' she said, 'Dr Noah is a great doctor. A few hours from now and this will all be over. When you get better you'll be able to do all those things you've always wanted to.'

Although Jack appreciated that his grandma was trying to make him feel better, he wished she would not; he just wanted to lay on the bed and look out the window. Jack's granddad entered the room at a sort of half run, as if he was worried he was late. He smiled at Jack and walked over to stare out the window.

Twenty minutes later the nurse returned.

'Jack it's time to go.'

Two porters came into the room with a bed on wheels and helped Jack onto it.

'Good luck, Jack,' Alan croaked, his voice threatening to break.

'We'll be waiting for you, sweetie,' Pam had added. 'We love you.'

'Love you too,' Jack said in small voice. 'See you soon.'

The porters pushed Jack through white corridors and white doors until they reached the theatre and they pushed Jack inside. Jack's perspective of the room was distorted because he was lying flat on his back, but he could see it was also white and very quiet. Jack was not able to see the machinery properly, which did not really matter because he would not have known what any of it was anyway. There were several people in the room, all dressed in standard green scrubs and wearing masks; they all turned and looked at Jack as he came in the room. Jack recognised Dr Noah who waved and walked towards Jack.

'Jackson, how are you feeling?' the doctor asked. His voice sounded loud in the unnaturally quiet room and almost echoey.

'Okay, I s'pose,' Jack replied in a strained voice he hardly recognised.

'Try not to worry,' Dr Noah said, 'it'll all be over soon,' and he touched Jack lightly on the shoulder.

Then a nurse, who was holding Jack's left hand, said, 'Jack, you will just feel a slight scratch,' as she pushed a needle into the back of Jack's hand. Then she added, 'Jack, if you could please count backwards from one hundred,'

'Okay,' Jack said in that strange voice again, his mouth getting drier every minute, 'One hundred, ninety-nine... ninety... eight...'

There was a sudden, heavy, irresistible sleepy feeling rushing through his body, and then everything went black.

2.

A New Life

The light was bright, too bright; Jack could not open his eyes properly because the light hurt them. He blinked rapidly a few times and tried to focus. Everything was white and blurry. He turned his head slowly to the left and tried to see where he was, through almost closed eyes he could just make out a window, but it was dark outside, he could also see a blurry bed and a chair with someone sitting in it. At his movement, the person sitting in the chair immediately got up and came towards him.

'Jack, can you hear me?' a woman's voice asked.

Yes, Jack could hear her, but he could not understand where he was or why his brain felt muzzy or why he could not get his mouth to move to speak. The woman spoke again.

'Jack, can you hear me? It's Tina, your nurse.'

His nurse? Why did he have a nurse? Nothing was making sense. Jack turned his head very slowly back the other way, he felt his eyes closing and he slipped back into unconsciousness.

When Jack's eyes opened again an hour later he felt a lot less muzzy, but a lot more pain. Every part of him hurt; he could not even blink without his eyes hurting, and he did not dare move his hand or head for fear of more pain. He wished someone would notice him this time and see that he was awake and maybe give him some painkillers or something. He tried to use his eyes to attract attention, he could see burry shapes moving around and wished one would look in his direction. Ages later, or so it seemed to Jack, someone walked over to his bed and looked down at him.

'Hey, sleepy head, how are you feeling?'

It sounded like the same woman who had spoken before, Tina? Jack only managed a dry croak.

'Thirsty?' She asked.

'Mm,' Jack groaned.

The woman disappeared and returned a short time later with a plastic cup full of water, she got a straw and put it to Jack's lips, the cold water felt wonderful in his dry mouth. She took the water and put it on the bedside table, then she moved to where a drip was hanging by the side of the bed, adjusted something and Jack felt his body go very heavy and everything went black again.

When Jack next awoke, the light at the window told him it was daytime. His eyesight and his mind were much clearer. He could see around the room, it looked like the same white room he had been in before. He could also remember a lot more. He could remember arriving at the hospital with Gran and Granddad. He could remember being pushed inside the operating theatre. He could even remember the pain in the back of his hand, counting backwards from one hundred and the immediate irresistible, heavy sleep that had overcome him. He could not remember anything after that until he had woken up in pain. As he looked around he noticed both his grandparents sleeping in chairs by his bed, he felt a sudden rush of love for his two most favourite people in the world. As he watched them Alan stirred and opened his eyes,

'Hey, son, how are you?' he asked.

This time Jack found his voice, 'Okay, I think... a bit sore,' that was an understatement.

Alan smiled, 'That's my boy, play it down, try not to move. I'll call the nurse.'

The talking woke Pam up, she immediately jumped to her feet and grabbed his hand and asked the same question her husband had. Before Alan had the chance to call the nurse, the door opened and Dr Noah entered the room. A tall elegant-looking man of about fifty, with grey-white hair and a thin moustache, Dr Noah had a presence that made everyone notice him when he moved and listen to him when he spoke.

'So, Jackson, how are you feeling?'

'Sore,' Jack croaked.

'Yes, I'm sure you are. Well the good news is that the operation went very well; I'm very pleased with you. The bad news is that you will feel sore for quite a while yet I'm afraid.'

Jack smiled weakly, Dr Noah returned the smile and continued, 'The next few days will be uncomfortable, I don't want you trying to do too much, you must take it easy and give your body a chance to heal. Obviously we need to keep a close eye on you, there are still things that can go wrong, but if you're good, I'm confident that you should be strong and ready to go home in a few weeks'.

So there it was, it was over, all the waiting, the preparation, the worry. The operation had gone well and if all continued that way, in a few weeks he would be strong enough to go home. Jack was not sure how he felt although relieved was high on the list.

Life in the hospital was pretty dull. Pam and Alan did everything to keep Jack comfortable and entertained, they spent all the time they could at Jack's bedside, playing games, reading books, anything to stop him being bored, but staying in bed all the time was tough. Sometimes he felt bad because he found it hard to hide his frustration and he often, without meaning to, snapped at them and hurt their feelings. He had a TV in the room and a DVD player, but daytime programmes were not very stimulating, (there are only so many episodes of *Jeremy Kyle* a guy can watch) and, although Pam insisted on bringing new DVD's every time she visited, Jack had already watched most of them several times. The times he looked forward to the most were the days Dennis visited. Dennis brought with him news of school – Eric was still hotly pursuing Katherine and Katherine, to Jack's great relief, was still saying no. The first time Dennis had seen post-op Jack he had been horrified, Jack had so many tubes coming out of him and he was so hooked up to machines that Dennis had got frightened for his friend. Jack had assured him that most of the stuff was just monitoring different parts of his body.

'Yikes, what does this do?' Dennis asked, pointing to the biggest machine in the room that was bleeping.

'That's monitoring my new heartbeat… to make sure it keeps going, I guess,' Jack had said, smiling.

'What's that tube sticking out of that bandage on your chest?' Dennis had asked.

'I think it's some sort of drain that takes the excess liquid away or something,' Jack had answered.

'Yuk!' Dennis had laughed, 'Sorry I asked, so why is there a needle sticking out of your hand?'

'They connect it to the drip when I need painkillers and stuff,' Jack explained.

'Oh,' said Dennis. 'So what's that on the inside of your arm?'

'What?' Jack had asked, looking at his right arm, 'What?'

'No, the other arm,' Dennis pointed to it.

Jack looked at his left arm, in the last few days since the operation he'd had so many pains in so many different parts of his body he had not noticed the light bandage around his left wrist covering what appeared to be a faint disc-shaped something.

'Dunno,' he admitted, touching it lightly. 'I never noticed it before... something else that monitors something I expect.'

Although it did not really bother him, Jack made a mental note to ask Dr Noah what the disc-thing was on his wrist next time he saw him, though with everything that was going on it slipped his mind until the day he was leaving the hospital.

Jack was running. Running very fast. Running through a field. The grass was very long and every so often there were clumps of bushes and nettles. The weather was overcast and it looked as though it would rain. Jack knew he was running away from something, although he had no idea what it was, he just knew he had to keep running. He also knew he was running towards something and that whatever it was would soon come into sight and he was desperate to see it. Jack was vaguely aware he was dreaming, he was aware he was having the same dream that he'd had before, but he was also aware there was a difference this time; he was barefoot, which not only did not seem weird to Jack, but actually seemed quite natural. Even though Jack was not wearing any shoes it did not slow him down, his feet, despite running over rocks and tree roots, felt no pain. As Jack's eyes tried to focus through the gloom, something started to come into focus, he started running faster, desperate to reach his goal, when he heard a voice,

'Jack, Jack, hey, son.'

Jack stopped running and looked up, he was in his bed in the hospital and his granddad was smiling down at him.

'Great news, son, Dr Noah says you can come home.'

Jack shook the sleep from his head and pulled himself into a sitting position, he looked from his granddad to Dr Noah and back again.

'Really? I can go home?' he asked eagerly.

'Yes, Jackson, I'm very impressed with your progress; I

think being in your own home will be better for you now. Try and get some normality back in your life,' Dr Noah said. 'Don't overdo it though,' he added quickly, smiling. 'You'll need to come back in a couple of days for us to check on you and you'll need to keep that bandage on your chest for a while, and the one on your wrist.'

'Oh yeah, Doctor, what is that on my wrist? Why do I have a bandage there?' Jack asked, suddenly remembering the disc-thing and looking from Dr Noah to his arm.

Dr Noah hesitated for just a second, 'It's just monitoring your pulse, making sure the pressure is maintained throughout your body, nothing to worry about,' Dr Noah assured him, though he looked slightly uncomfortable.

'Okay, I guessed it would be something like that,' Jack replied and put it from his mind.

So three weeks after the operation Jack found himself back at home, back in the house he shared with his grandparents. Jack was very glad to be home, the hospital had a funny smell and, although it was comfortable, it just was not the same as being in your own house with all your own things around you, and, most of all, sleeping in your own bed. Dr Noah had warned him that he would feel weak and tired for quite a while and to take things easy. Pam and Alan fussed and worried over him. They did not let him do anything for himself; they waited on him hand and foot.

Dennis tried to visit every day after school; he had gone to the hospital as often as he could but he did not feel comfortable there and was much happier now Jack was home. He also would not allow Jack to do anything or lift anything when he was there, scuttling around like a mini Pam.

Jack was desperate for news of school. He had missed so much, including the exams, and he was terribly behind in every subject. He was also feeling bad that poor Dennis was getting all of Eric's unwanted attention with Jack not around and he knew how hard it was to deal with Eric on your own. Dennis had been round the day before and told him of Eric's latest game.

'He waits every day at the school gate for me to arrive, he takes my bag, steals my lunch money and my homework. I'm in trouble with Mr Harvey, Mrs Neville and Mr Cowper, as they all think I haven't been doing my homework, but I have, Eric just rips it up. I've got a lot of detentions, it's so unfair.'

Anyone who had not been the subject of bullying might not understand why Dennis just did not tell someone, his parents or one of the teachers, but Jack understood: telling would only make Eric worse.

Jack was also desperate for news of Katherine, but he found it hard to ask Dennis, what would he ask? He was worried that Katherine might have given in to Eric and that when he did eventually get back to school she would no longer smile at him.

To Jack's great delight and relief Poppy came visiting the day he got home. He had been worried that she might have given up on him after finding him not there for so many days running. She seemed to know that something was wrong with Jack, however, and she was even more careful than usual.

'Cats have a sixth sense when it comes to things like this,' Pam had told him seriously, 'they seem to know when people are sick or sad.'

Jack watched as Poppy carefully and lightly jumped up onto the settee next to him and settled into her usual position, curled up in a ball. He stroked her head and back and she started purring, he smiled feeling happier than he had for days.

The thing that slightly bothered Jack, and he was not really sure why, was, despite Dr Noah's warning that he would feel weak and tired, he actually did not feel in the least bit weak or tired at all, in fact, he had never felt better, literally never. He felt like he could do anything. He assumed that he was feeling well because he was resting so much and that if he tried to get up and move around he would probably then feel weak and tired. He also no longer felt sick or out of breath; he put this down to the new drugs he was taking and this meant that his appetite improved beyond recognition, much to the delight of Pam, who liked nothing better than spending many hours slaving away in the kitchen cooking. Jack tried to act a bit sick though, he did not want anyone to know how good he was feeling because he was sure he should not feel quite this good quite so quickly. Something else he had noticed was he seemed to have a highly elevated sense of smell. As he walked slowly around the house he could identify each different cleaning product Pam had used: furniture polish, bathroom cleaner, bleach, they smelled very strongly in his nose and the bleach actually felt like it was burning. The cooking smells that wafted in from the kitchen were much stronger than he had ever noticed before. Jack found it a little strange that he could smell raw food just as strongly as cooked food and, weirdly, they were just as appetising. The one thing he could not hide though, was how good he was looking. His pale skin no longer looked so pale and he was sure he was putting on weight, probably due to the amount of food he was eating.

By the time Jack had the all clear to go back to school, he had been back to the hospital for several check-ups. He had been intrigued to see the scar on his chest the first time they had removed the bandage to check on his healing, expecting it to be about six inches long, he had been shocked that it was almost twice that length. Angry and sore, it had looked like a thick, red worm winding its way down his body and he had wondered if it would always look like that. He had also been shocked when the nurse had removed the bandage on his arm, expecting to see a small disc somehow stuck to his wrist, he had been horrified to see the disc was under his skin. He could see his veins pulsing around it. It was about the size and shape of a two pound coin and it raised and stretched the skin as if there was not really enough room for it. Touching it lightly with the fingers of his right hand he was surprised to feel it vibrating slightly. It still felt and looked very alien to Jack and he had been even more shocked when he had asked how long he would have to have the disc under his skin for.

'Forever,' the nurse had replied, a bit abruptly.

Jack's mouth had fallen open as he stared first at the nurse and then at his arm. Seeing the look on Jack's face, she smiled, 'Don't worry, love, you'll get used to it. You won't notice it after a while, and it's doing a very important job.'

Jack nodded, almost without knowing he was doing it, he doubted he would ever be able to forget that thing was there; it looked so weird and the skin appeared to be so tightly stretched across it, it looked as though it would easily tear. Shuddering slightly, Jack had tried to put it to the back of his mind.

Jack's first day back at school arrived after a mere two weeks at home, Dr Noah had been very surprised, but pleased, with Jack's rapid progress, saying he had never seen anyone heal as fast. Even Jack, despite knowing that he felt fine even when he did move around, was surprised on his last check-up to see that the scar on his chest had changed dramatically. It was no longer red and angry looking, it was almost the same colour as the rest of his skin and was just a thin line, rather than the worm it had been before. The disc inserted under the skin of Jack's left wrist still bothered him, not because it hurt – it did not, it had even stopped itching for a while – it still bothered him because he could not get used to the way it looked – it just looked so weird. Jack made a mental note to find some form of clothing that would cover his wrist without drawing attention to it, so he would not have to look at it.

Dr Noah had also been surprised to find that Jack's body no longer seemed to require any drugs, so Jack had stopped taking them a week before going back to school. Not only were there no adverse effects, but Jack actually felt even better than he had before, although he would not have believed that possible. Jack was now very aware that he had changed physically; he had spent a lot of time in front of the mirror in the bathroom studying his reflection, something he had always avoided before. His skin, once so pale now had a normal healthy look, almost a glow. His hair was shiny and his eyes seemed to twinkle. He had also definitely gained weight and this had given him a new, healthy, almost powerful look, which he assumed he had inherited from his granddad, but had never realised before because of his illness. He had been forced to go shopping with Pam to get new clothes because none of his fitted anymore. While Pam had been distracted, he had slipped some wristbands onto the shopping pile. Best of all, Jack was still feeling so good; he felt as though he could do anything these days, anything. The thought of actually running, and not just dreaming about running, no longer bothered Jack. In fact, he longed to try it.

Dennis was of course delighted to have his friend back, not just because he missed having Jack around, but also because it meant he no longer had to deal with Eric on his own. Jack was not looking forward to seeing Eric and was disappointed to almost bump into him in the first ten minutes of his first day back at school. Jack had been standing outside the classroom, talking to Dennis, waiting for the first lesson to start, when Eric had come sauntering up behind him saying.

'Hey, look who's back,' Eric had commented with a sound of evil delight. He had just opened his mouth to make another comment when Jack turned around to face him. Eric's mouth had remained open, but no sound had come out. The look on his face told Jack that he was shocked at his appearance, and could not think of anything nasty to say. Once they had entered the classroom and sat down, Jack realised that Dennis was staring at him.

'What?' Jack asked puzzled.

'I never noticed before, but you've changed,' said Dennis still staring.

'Changed?' Jack asked, 'How?'

'You're bigger,' Dennis replied, 'and your face…'

'My face, what?' asked Jack.

'Your face looks different,' Dennis said thoughtfully, 'more round and not so… I don't know… white.'

Eric and Dennis were not the only ones to notice the difference in Jack. Jack was sure that he was getting looks from most of the other students and they were not the usual looks of pity or distaste, these were looks of amazement and, in some cases, he could have sworn they were looks of admiration.

From the reactions so far, he was desperate to bump into Katherine; for the first few days after his return he did not see her, then, finally, towards the end of his first week he spotted her, alone as usual, sitting on a wall by the front gate. He took a detour so he had to walk past her. As he neared, he noticed a light and very appealing scent that seemed to come from her direction, she seemed to sense his approach and looked up, she smiled, her usual smile. To Jack's surprise, though, there was no look of shock or surprise at his appearance, it was as though this was the Jack she had always known or she had seen him this way before.

Jack was careful at school not to draw too much attention to himself. Everyone had noticed that the skinny, pale, ill kid was suddenly no longer skinny or pale or ill; in fact, they realised that he was broad, bordering on muscular, and was looking positively healthy. Jack thought it best not to show off his new found energy too soon. Though he longed to join in with sports, his teachers did not expect him to and he had never been able to before; following his major heart surgery, they were surprised to see him back at school, let alone exercising. So Jack maintained his 'nothing physical' status and kept Dennis company doing extra lessons instead. Once out of school though, he felt unable to constrain his energy. Living near the Ashdown Forest, there were a lot of places to walk and ride bikes. Every day after school Jack would go home, change out of his uniform and head for one of the forest walks. After school was a quiet time in these places with weekends and early mornings being the most popular time to walk dogs, so Jack often had them to himself. Jack had started by setting himself targets and walking for ten minutes the first day, then twenty minutes the second day. After a few weeks he started running, well jogging really. Again he started with just ten minutes and so on. Eventually he was running, really running, and he just never seemed to get tired or worn out. Jack would run, and run, and run. It felt so good to just run, it felt free; after being trapped in a useless frail body, to have a body with so much energy was wonderful. This newfound energy did not exactly bother Jack, on the contrary, he was very grateful for it, but it did make him wonder. Dr Noah had never told him to expect to feel like this, he had never warned him that he would be bouncing off the walls with excess energy, he had never mentioned that he might feel more lively than before. This made Jack wonder whether it was normal. In fact, thinking about everything that had happened since the operation, the extraordinarily fast healing, the energy, the weight, the skin colour, made Jack think that, maybe, none of what was happening to him was normal. That said, they were all positive things and therefore nothing to complain about.

3.

THE STRANGE GIFT

A few weeks after Jack's return to school, Christmas loomed and there was a lot of excited talk in the corridors about the school party. Everyone was going, all the girls were talking about what they were going to wear and most of the boys were wondering if they would get caught if they tried to smuggle cider in. Jack and Dennis had always avoided the party before; being the least popular kids in school, they had always assumed it would just be like an extension of lessons and they would be tormented. Now, however, Jack found himself considering it. He would not say Eric had laid off completely since Jack's return to school but certainly there had been a lot less attention their way. Whether this was down to the fact that they were in their exam year and Eric was studying harder (though this did seem quite unlikely), or whether it had something to do with the fact that Jack was almost as big as Eric now, Jack did not know, but he was not complaining.

One day when they were walking to English, Jack broached the subject with Dennis.

'Den?' he asked, 'What do you reckon to going to the Christmas party?'

To Jack's surprise, Dennis said, 'Yeah, I've been thinking about that.'

'You have?' Jack asked sounding surprised.

'Yeah, think it might be a laugh,' Dennis had added, ''bout time we got ourselves a social life.' And with that he walked into class, leaving Jack looking stunned behind him. There had to be more to this than Dennis was letting on.

Two weeks later, Jack and Dennis found themselves standing in line to be let into the school hall for the party. The place had been decorated with a very large tree covered in tinsel and baubles and there were garlands festooned all over the walls. Right in the centre of the room someone had hung a huge bunch of mistletoe, held together with a large red ribbon. Everyone seemed to know it was there and avoided standing under it.

Jack and Dennis helped themselves to a Coke each and started wandering around the hall, boys were lined up against the walls chatting and watching the girls who were dancing to the music. Jack looked around the hall hoping to see Katherine when he noticed Dennis was staring at someone right over the other side of the room; a small, dark-haired girl, who was wearing a black shimmery dress and black shiny sandals. She seemed not only aware that Dennis was staring at her, but she appeared to be staring back.

'Who's that girl?' Jack asked, looking from Dennis to the girl and back again.

Dennis blushed, 'Bryony Fielding,' he replied, a little sheepishly.

'Do you know her?' Jack asked.

'Not really,' Dennis answered, 'she spoke to me once in history. She asked me what a date was or something.'

'Oh,' said Jack. Rather than point out Dennis was staring at Bryony and therefore embarrass his friend, Jack said, 'She's staring at you.'

'Do you think so?' Dennis asked eagerly. 'I was thinking

about asking her to dance actually, what do you think?'

Jack was surprised at his friend's honesty, he himself had liked Katherine for ages, but had never admitted it to anyone and would have denied it if he had been asked.

'Dunno,' he said, 'can you dance?'

'Not very well,' Dennis admitted, 'I danced once at my cousin's wedding... but it was with my Mum,' he added, laughing.

'Well you go for it if that's what you want.'

'Hmm, not really that easy though, is it?' said Dennis thoughtfully, 'I mean, she always smiles at me, so I think she likes me, but, well, you never know, do you?'

'No,' agreed Jack. 'You never know'

They stood chatting and drinking their Cokes for a while then Jack knew Katherine had entered the room as he smelled her unmistakable sweet perfume. He turned around in time to see her walking slowly towards an empty table furthest away from the dance floor where she sat alone. He watched as both girls and boys approached her and either stayed and chatted for a while or left fairly quickly, but none stayed long. Katherine spent most of the time alone. Jack's new heart started beating very fast every time he looked over at her and found her looking at him, it beat even faster each time he thought about going over and talking to her or asking her to dance, but he could not find the courage to do either.

The rest of the evening Jack and Dennis chatted to each other, they laughed as they watched people dancing, though Jack's eyes were never far from Katherine's direction, and Dennis wondered aloud again whether he should speak to Bryony.

'What's the worst that can happen?' he reasoned, 'I mean, if I ask her and she says no I haven't really lost anything, have I? I mean, apart from the fact that I'll feel like a fool, my life will be over and I'll never be able to face anyone at school again, not a lot to give up is it?'

Jack laughed, 'Actually we have both always looked like fools, we've never even had a life and no one at school even notices us, so no it's not a lot to give up!'

They both laughed.

'I do know how you feel,' Jack said deciding the time had come to confess to Dennis, 'I'd like to ask someone to dance, not that I can dance,' he added quickly.

'Yeah I know,' said Dennis draining his glass and pointing across the room, 'Katherine Felix.'

'Er, yes, how'd you know?'

'Not hard, mate, I've seen the way you watch her. Also, when you were off school, you were only ever interested when I mentioned her – your eyes glazed over when I talked about anything else.' Dennis thought for a while, 'Reckon she likes you, you know. She's always looking at you and she smiles at you, doesn't she?'

'Yeah, but like you said,' Jack said. 'You never know.'

'No,' agreed Dennis, 'You never know.'

The next morning, when Jack awoke, he was in his bed laying on his left side, he rolled onto his back, blinking in the daylight, and yelped in pain. He quickly rolled back onto his side; something hard was in his bed. He groped around with his right hand to see what it was but could not feel anything. He rolled gingerly this time onto his back and cried out in pain again. Carefully he raised himself up to a sitting position and felt his back, at the base of his spine was a lump, a big lump, no, not a lump, more a stump really. It was about an inch across and about an inch long and it was very tender to touch. Jack leaped out of bed and raced to his bathroom. Standing with his back to the mirror he pulled up his pyjama top and turned his head so he could see over his shoulder and stared at the place he had felt the stump. There was definitely something sticking out of his skin – no, not sticking out of his skin, more like it was *growing* out of his skin, really. He turned his head to the front and then back again at the mirror expecting the hallucination to have finished, but the stump was still there. He sat down carefully on the toilet seat; his heart was beating very fast and his breath was very rapid, he needed to calm down or he would bring on a panic attack. Horrible pills making him see things, playing tricks on his mind, he thought. But a scared little part of his brain reminded him that he was not taking any pills, he had not taken any pills for months, so it could not be them to blame. Trying to push this from his mind he decided he must be tired. He climbed back into bed, carefully avoiding touching the base of his spine to the bed and rolled onto his left side. When he awoke an hour later to his gran calling him, everything was once again back to normal.

Christmas was a happy time in the King house. Pam and Alan were so relieved that the operation was over and done with and the results were so excellent that they decided to go over the top with the Christmas celebrations. Pam went crazy, covering every spare inch of the house she could find with tinsel and baubles and nagged until Alan found the ladder to hang lights up outside, although Alan insisted they were less exuberant than the lights inside. They spent a fortune on Jack's presents, Christmas morning found Jack opening an iPhone, an iPad, a Wii with loads of games, scores of DVD's and CD's and more chocolate than he could ever hope to eat. But the present Jack liked best was the racing bike. He had never had a bike before: most kids get them as soon as they could walk, but with Jack's heart problem he had never had enough energy. Now he stared at the shiny black two-wheeler and imagined the freedom he would feel. Of course, never having had a bike, he had never learned to ride one. He knew he would find it frustrating having to learn, but Alan had promised that he would start the lessons the day after Boxing Day and Jack could not wait.

Christmas Day evening, Pam and Alan had invited some friends around for drinks so Jack had invited Dennis. Dennis was full of it when he arrived. They were in Jack's bedroom.

'Got some great stuff this year,' he said, shovelling handfuls of chocolate in his mouth and showing Jack his new mobile phone.

'Look, it has some great features,' and he started flicking through the phone's menu.

They exchanged numbers and sent silly texts to each other. When Jack told Dennis he had got a bike, Dennis laughed and said he also had a bike, but had never really used it.

'Mum thought it might do me some good to get out and get some fresh air,' he explained, 'never really bothered with it, might dig it out now you have one, though, could be a laugh.'

At that moment, Pam called from downstairs.

'Boys, the guests are arriving, are you ever coming down to say hello and get a drink?'

They both got up and reluctantly went downstairs, preferring to stay out of the way. People were milling around all over the place, most of them Jack recognised as his grandparents' friends and neighbours. People he had known all his life and yet did not really know at all. He and Dennis went through to the kitchen, a large open room fitted with pine cabinets and a large island in the middle from which Alan was serving drinks.

'Any chance of a beer, Granddad?' Jack asked smiling.

Alan looked at his grandson, 'I think I can find one, it is Christmas after all... lager for you as well, Dennis?' He asked.

'Yes, please, Mr King,' Dennis answered eagerly.

The boys took their drinks and moved into the lounge,

it was nearly full. How many people had his grandparents invited? Looking around he was surprised to see Dr Noah there; he was talking to a girl who had her back to Jack. Dr Noah spotted Jack, waved and started toward him, the girl turned around to see who the doctor was waving at and Jack was shocked to see it was Katherine. What was she doing in his house with Dr Noah? He nudged Dennis who had been looking the other way; Dennis gaped at Katherine for a second.

'What's she doing here?' he asked, 'and who's that bloke she's with?'

'That's my doctor from the hospital,' Jack replied, surprised Dennis had never seen him before, 'but I have no idea what Katherine's doing with him.'

Dr Noah approached Jack saying, 'Hi, Jackson. Happy Christmas, how are you?'

'Er, happy Christmas. I'm fine actually, thanks,' Jack replied, very conscious of his own voice.

Dr Noah looked at Katherine.

'Jackson, you know Katherine, don't you?'

'Hi, Jack,' she said.

'Er, hi,' said Jack through a very dry mouth, he look a swig of lager and spilled some down his chin. He tried to mop it up without anyone seeing, as he dragged his hand across his mouth, he froze. He felt and saw that his hand had long, black hairs growing on it. Dropping his lager he mumbled something that sounded a bit like, 'Excuse me,' and raced from the room.

He ran upstairs and into his bathroom, panting wildly, he locked the door. He sat down on the toilet seat, his heart pounding and looked down at his hand. He sat looking at it in stunned silence, oblivious to the people outside the bathroom knocking and shouting at him to open the door. How long he sat there he was not sure. He tried not to panic thinking this would only make things worse. He closed his eyes, praying that when he opened them again the hairs would be gone and his hand would be back to normal. Assuring himself that no one else would have shared in his hallucination, that he was the only one who could see them, he wondered what they were all thinking as to why he had run from the room. Looking down he saw hair was now covering the backs of both his hands. It was thick and coarse and dark and quite dense in places. He closed his eyes again and took some very deep breaths and could feel himself calming down slightly, he opened his eyes and peeked at his hands, he thought the hair was getting a little bit thinner. He closed his eyes again, this time he was aware of the people outside the door. He could hear his grandparents' voices and Dennis'.

'Sorry,' he called, 'I'm fine, just felt a bit sick, I'll be down in a minute.' His voice sounded strained.

'Sweetie,' Pam said, 'let us in, darling, we're worried about you.'

'Really, Gran, I'm fine. I'll be down soon,' he called back.

He heard footsteps moving away from the door and relaxed a bit more, looking at his hands, they were almost back to normal. He stood up and went to the sink, he washed his face and when he looked back at his hands he was relieved to see the hallucination had completely gone.

Ten minutes later he was back downstairs, apologising for spilling his beer and assuring everyone that he was fine.

'Really, I'm fine,' he kept insisting, 'I just felt a bit sick.'

However, the look he was getting from Dr Noah told him not everyone believed him.

The New Year started with a light smattering of snow. Jack was walking into the hospital for his check up with Dr Noah. He went up to the third floor and told the receptionist he was there, he was surprised to be sent straight through. He knocked on the door of Dr Noah's office.

'Come in,' he heard the doctor's voice.

Jack entered the familiar room.

'Sit down,' Dr Noah said.

Jack sat. Dr Noah looked at Jack for a few seconds before speaking, finally he said, 'So, Jackson, how are you?'

'Fine,' Jack replied.

Dr Noah studied him again for a few seconds.

'How are you really?' he asked.

'Fine,' repeated Jack.

'So what was all that about on Christmas Day?' the doctor asked.

Jack had been expecting this question and dreading it.

'Nothing,' he lied, 'I just felt sick.'

'Can't take you're beer, eh?' Dr Noah joked.

'Something like that,' Jack replied.

Dr Noah went silent again and Jack started to feel uncomfortable. He looked around the room, wishing the doctor would say something. Eventually the doctor did speak.

'Jackson, I can't help if you don't tell me what's wrong.'

Jack started, did Dr Noah know about Jack's hallucinations?

'There's nothing to tell,' Jack assured him, but, before he could continue, Dr Noah finished for him.

'You just felt sick, I get it.'

They looked at each other and Dr Noah said, 'Okay, well if there's nothing you want to tell me, I'll just get on with the physical examination.'

Ten minutes later, with a clean bill of health, Jack was heading back out of the hospital to where Alan was waiting in the car listening to the football on the radio.

When Jack got home from the hospital he phoned Dennis.

'Hey, Den, wanna go out on the bikes?' He asked.

'Okay, be round in ten,' Dennis answered.

Jack had taken to riding a bike like a fish to water – it was easy. He had no problem with the balance and, even though his first attempt had been a bit wobbly, he had not fallen off and now, two weeks later, was riding like a pro. Dennis was not as confident on the bike as Jack; he had not ridden in a long time and was a bit off balance.

Dennis arrived at Jack's house half an hour later.

'Sorry I'm late,' he had spluttered, 'Mum wouldn't let me leave until I'd eaten something,' he rolled his eyes.

'You're here now,' said Jack, 'let's get going.'

They both got on their bikes and headed off towards one of the forest walks. The trails were quite uneven in places, a bit bumpy, so Dennis did not like going too fast. Jack would ride on ahead and then double back and meet Dennis, who was pootling along quite happily. The weather was lovely for the time of year and Jack felt he could ride forever. On this particular occasion, Jack was several hundred feet in front of Dennis when his bike hit a pothole, skidded on a patch of snow and he lost control, sending the bike careering into a tree. Jack toppled off the bike onto the hard earth, striking his arm against the tree trunk.

'Ow,' he moaned out loud and looked at his arm, it was bloody and his jumper was torn, 'Damn,' he swore and tried to get up. Only then did he notice that there was something wrong with his right leg. It was not injured, but there was something wrong. It hurt and it looked, well, thinner and longer, as he looked at it he could see it getting longer, sticking further and further out the bottom of his jeans. Dennis caught up with him and got off his bike.

'You alright?' he asked, then looking at Jack's arm, 'Yikes, bet that hurts.'

'Yes it does,' admitted Jack, 'and Gran will freak when she sees this jumper, it's new.'

Dennis looked puzzled.

'What's up with your leg?' he asked.

Jack froze, Dennis could see his leg? He had assumed he was having a hallucination.

'What do you mean?' Jack asked, playing dumb.

'Your leg', Dennis pointed at it, 'it looks funny... oh no, it doesn't. Oh, er, must have been the light or the angle or something...'

Jack looked back at his leg and Dennis was right, it was back to normal. But Dennis had seen something. Jack did not know much about hallucinations, but he did know two people could not see the same one at the same time.

'Think I'd better go home, Den.' Jack said. 'Get this cleaned up,' and he pointed to his arm.

'Yeah, course,' Dennis said.

They set off for home, but Jack was feeling uneasy; something was not right here, if what he was suffering from were not hallucinations and, if Dennis could see them, they could not be hallucinations, then what was wrong with him? And, if they were not hallucinations, then was all this weird stuff really happening to him, not just the leg getting longer and thinner but the hair and the stump at the base of his spine? And if all this stuff was really happening, what on earth did it all mean, what was happening to him?

By the time Jack got home, the cut on his arm had healed; there was only dried blood and the hole in his jumper left to show anything had happened at all.

The 11th February was rapidly approaching once they were into the New Year. Pam and Alan kept asking Jack what he wanted for this birthday; they wanted to make a fuss, after all it was his seventeenth. But Jack really could not tell them what he wanted: to stop having this weird stuff happen to him, to remove the horrible disc-thing from under his skin which had started itching again and sometimes kept him awake at night vibrating, and to have a date with Katherine. He settled in the end for driving lessons, but he could not have them yet; Dr Noah had told him that he needed a whole year of good health before he would be given the okay to learn to drive, so Pam and Alan said they would pay for lessons as soon as Jack was able to start. Dennis, whose birthday was in November and was already seventeen, had already started driving lessons.

'Great fun, mate,' he would tell Jack after each one, 'I'm learning really fast, I should be passing my test soon, then there's no stopping us, I'm gonna get a car. Not a brand new car, it'll have to be quite old and not too powerful or it'll cost a fortune in insurance, but, hey, it'll still be a car. I'm saving already.' Dennis had a Saturday job at a garden centre and was saving every penny for his car. He looked thoughtful for a moment and then added, 'Do you think Bryony will like me better when I can drive?'

Jack looked at him, 'Dunno,' he said.

So far neither of them had managed to ask out the girl of their choice; opportunities just did not present themselves very often, school was not the right place at all. Eric was much quieter these days, Jack wondered if perhaps he had found a new victim and was using up all his energy there, although he still saw Eric staring sometimes, and it was never a good look.

Jack and Dennis had discussed the possibility of Jack having a party for his birthday but they did not have enough friends between them to make a party and really they would only want to invite two people.

Jack was dreaming again, he was running, running very fast. He was streaking through a town, a blur. He was running towards something, but he just could not see what it was, he was running through streets. He knew what he was running to was just ahead. He slowed slightly, avoiding bins and seats and streetlamps on the pavement. Keeping a steady pace, he looked from side to side to ensure there was nothing else in his way.

His eye caught something and he stopped almost instantly. Looking at a shop to his left, he moved slowly towards the window, staring not at what was on the other side of the glass, but at his own reflection; he did not look like himself at all. He was shorter, stockier and his back was slightly arched. It was hard to tell in the shop window, but his face looked quite hairy, as though he had a long, full beard and his arms were long, far too long. There was also something long and thin hanging from his back, like he had a rope tied round his waist and it was hanging down almost to the ground, as if he had been tied to something and had escaped. Jack awoke with a start, staring at the ceiling. He could remember the dream clearly. He got out of bed and went into his bathroom wearing only his pyjama bottoms; he wondered vaguely what had happened to his top. Looking in the mirror, he was shocked to see he was still dreaming, his reflection was the same as he had seen in the shop window in his sleep. Blinking twice he splashed his face with cold water and looked in the mirror again and this time when he looked at himself, he was awake.

School was not going so well for Jack. He had missed so much when he had been in hospital that it was hard to catch up; he was drowning in homework and was thinking he would never be ready for his exams. He had missed his GCSE's when he had been ill and had stayed on to take them the following year. He had tried bringing up the subject of leaving school with his grandparents but they would not hear of it.

'You need some qualifications, sweetie,' Pam had said, 'you can't just drop out without at least taking your exams.'

Alan had backed her up, 'Not a chance, son,' he had said sternly. 'You'll never get a job if you don't get qualifications.'

So Jack had no choice but to carry on.

Sitting in his room, surrounded by mountains of books and papers, he was staring blankly at a piece of paper, not reading or taking in anything written on it. He looked at his watch, it was eight o'clock. Feeling tired and fed up he decided to leave the homework for the evening and continue tomorrow. Tomorrow being Saturday, he could devote more time to work when his head was fresher. Pushing his chair away from his desk, he was just about to switch on his TV when Pam shouted up the stairs.

'Jack. Sweetie, someone is here to see you.'

Jack went downstairs to the front door and was greeted by a skinny man, wearing tatty, dirty clothes and a worried expression. He had bright blue eyes that darted around and he was hopping from one foot to the other, as though he was afraid of something or desperate for the loo. He looked at Jack as he approached, without speaking, he pulled a small, roughly-packaged parcel out of his pocket and thrust it at Jack. Jack only just had time to grab it before the man took off at a run. Jack stood at the front door for a few minutes not sure what to make of what had just happened; eventually he closed the door and went back upstairs. He sat down on his bed and looked at the package, it was about six inches square and wrapped, badly, in tatty brown paper. Jack was not sure whether he should open it or not – who had that strange man been and why would anyone be giving him a present, if that's what it was? After a while of staring at it, Jack decided he would open it; he ripped the paper off and found an old black leather box with the word *Moraid* embossed in pealing gold leaf across the top. Jack stared at the word, but could make no sense of it. He opened the box and inside there was a piece of paper. Jack took it out and looked at it, it had one word hand-written in an untidy scrawl on it, *Ski*, and underneath the paper was what looked like a metal tube nestled in the dark red velvet lining. Jack took it out of the box and looked at it carefully; it was silvery in colour and looked quite old and tarnished, it was about three inches wide and solid like a sort of bangle. It was hinged down one side and had a strong looking padlock and key to keep it secure when it was closed. On the inside, in a large fancy script, two letters had been engraved: *CJ*. Jack had never seen anything like it before, what on earth was it? Some sort of jewellery, or perhaps part of a suit of armour? Whatever it was, Jack did not think it had anything to do with skiing. Although with the tough-looking hinge and the strong-looking lock, it definitely looked functional rather than decorative. Jack had no idea what it was or why someone would give it to him; perhaps it had not been meant for him at all, perhaps the strange man had mistaken him for someone else. He looked at it for a little longer and went to put it back in the box when he noticed something else, almost hidden in the folds of the velvet. He reached in and pulled out what looked like a thimble. He twisted it around in his fingers, looking at it from every angle; it was silver in colour with an ornate pattern carved into the metal and set with tiny coloured stones. Again Jack was puzzled, why would anyone give him a thimble? He placed in back in the box with the bangle-thing and tossed the box into one of his drawers.

The next Monday at school Jack had trouble concentrating on any of his subjects; the metal bangle-thing and the thimble kept bothering him. Why, he kept asking himself. Why, would someone go the trouble of delivering a package and not explaining what it was or who it was from or why? And just what did *Moraid* and *Ski* mean? It just did not make any sense. He did not tell Dennis about it, he did not think Dennis would have any better idea than he did. He just could not get it out of his mind. When at last the bell rang for home time, Jack was still puzzling over it as he started to walk out of the school gates. As he started walking towards the bus stop to get the bus home, however, something happened that drove the metal bangle-thing, the thimble and the strange words completely out of his head. He spotted Katherine on the other side of the road. As he looked at her, she saw him and raised her left arm to wave at him. He was about to wave back when he froze, the sun had caught the skin of Katherine's arm at just the right angle; staring at her, Jack saw, quite clearly, there on her wrist, under the skin, a disc shaped something that was about the size and shape of a two pound coin.

4.

KATHERINE FELIX

Jack stood frozen to the spot, unable to move or wave or anything. His mind was racing; Katherine had a disc under the skin on her left wrist, just like he had, what did that mean? Had she also had heart surgery and her pulse was being monitored? How long had she had it? Why had he never noticed it before? Katherine stopped waving and looked puzzled at his non-response. He shook his head to try to clear it and realised she was still staring at him, he quickly waved back, but she was no longer smiling and had started walking away. He longed to follow her, his mind was full of unanswered questions, but she was walking away very quickly and he realised he had missed his chance. Walking slowly towards the bus stop, he was angry with himself; why had he not just taken control and walked over and spoken to her, had she not made it obvious enough that she liked him? Even if like was all she felt, surely she would not ignore him if he spoke to her. It was not like they did not have anything in common to talk about: they both went to the same school, they both disliked Eric, at least Jack did, and Katherine never looked very keen whenever he was around, they both knew Dr Noah and they both had disc-things under their skin, surely that was enough to get them started. Jack made a decision: it was time to stop messing around and get to know Katherine Felix. How, he was not sure, he decided to enlist Dennis' help.

'Dunno, mate' Dennis said when Jack rang him later that evening and asked him how he should get talking to Katherine, 'You know me. I've never been able to talk to girls, look at me and Bryony. I've only ever said about five words to her in about as many months and most of them I stuttered.'

'Well, I need some sort of plan,' complained Jack, 'I can't just stumble up to her and start talking rubbish, she'll think I'm an idiot.'

'You are an idiot,' said Dennis laughing, 'but that shouldn't stop you.' He added, only slightly more seriously, 'You're right, we need a plan.'

But needing a plan and coming up with one were two very different things and, wrack their brains though they might, they could not come up with anything that would not make Jack look and feel foolish. They speculated over double dates, fake reasons to have a party and accidently-on-purpose bumping into her near her house (although they were not entirely sure where she lived). They tried to think of places she might go; shopping on a Saturday perhaps, though, didn't girls tend to do that with other girls?

'Soph never shops alone,' Dennis confirmed wisely, 'she always has one or both of the twins with her, they need each other's opinion or something.'

Also Jack was not keen on hanging round girly shops on his own. They wondered about clubs or social gatherings she might attend, but she was always such a loner at school that it seemed unlikely she would be into that sort of thing. Dennis even suggested they try going to the library in town to see if she went there though again it was a long shot. Luckily for Jack the perfect opportunity presented itself just a few days later.

Jack was at Dr Noah's office having his monthly check up. He had been surprised and pleased that his scar had, in the last few weeks, almost completely disappeared. You could just see a faint line if the light was at the right angle, but really it was hardly there at all. Even Dr Noah seemed mildly surprised at Jack's rapid healing. Jack was still bothered by the disc-thing and, remembering Katherine's wrist, he asked Dr Noah, 'Is it only people who've had heart transplants that have these disc-things under their skin?'

Dr Noah seemed surprised at the question, 'Why do you ask?'

'Just wondered,' Jack replied. 'Just wondered how many other people have them.'

'No,' replied the doctor. 'It's not only people who have heart transplants that need the discs, there could be a number of reasons.'

'Like what?' asked Jack.

Dr Noah looked at Jack without speaking for a while. Finally he said. 'A number of reasons, Jackson, too many to go into now.'

Jack knew he had been fobbed off and was sure the doctor was looking a bit uncomfortable.

'Well, once again you have a clean bill of health,' the doctor continued, 'anything bothering you Jackson? Any problems? Anything you want to discuss with me?'

'No,' replied Jack, 'I'm fine.'

'Fine then. I'll see you in a month.' And with that the doctor looked down at his notes and started writing; Jack recognised the dismissal.

He left the doctor's office and was walking down the corridor, towards the door. The hospital was in Tenbridge so he would need to get the bus, but, looking at his watch, he realised he had a good thirty minutes before one was due. He was walking along slowly, trying to kill some time, looking at the floor and wondering why Dr Noah did not want to talk about the disc when someone bumped into him.

'Sorry,' he muttered, looking up into the face of Katherine Felix. 'Hi,' he said quickly, feeling himself start to redden.

'Hi, Jack,' she said, smiling, her startling eyes twinkling, 'Just been to see the doc?'

'Yeah,' he confirmed. 'You?'

'Sort of,' she smiled, and started towards the doctor's office.

'Wait,' Jack almost shouted.

She turned around, slightly startled and looked at him questioningly.

'I mean, er, sorry, I mean hi.' He was getting redder by the minute.

She laughed softly.

'What do you mean Jack?' she asked, her eyes twinkling.

'Um, dunno,' Jack stammered. 'Sorry.' He felt very foolish and turned to go.

'I'm not going to be long,' she offered kindly, 'if you're not in a hurry perhaps we could go for a coffee in the canteen?'

Jack stared at her stupidly for a second and then blurted, 'What? Yeah, great, er, yeah.'

She smiled, 'Okay, see you in a bit.' And she disappeared into the doctor's outer office.

Jack stood frozen to the spot; he had a date with Katherine, well, no, not really a date, but he did have a… what, sort of date… ish thing. Anyway, he would finally get to talk to her without anyone else around. Oh no, what was he going to say? He hung around in the corridor trying to calm his pounding heart and feeling very hot. His stomach felt as though it was about to regurgitate his lunch. He felt a sudden pain in his finger. *Oh no, not now*, he thought, *please don't let me have one of those hallucination things now*. But the honest part of his brain that liked to point out all those things he hated to admit, reminded him that they were not hallucinations – Dennis had seen the last one, had he not? And if he did not get a grip on himself, Katherine might witness this one.

Ten minutes later, Jack, having forced himself to take deep breaths and therefore avoid the hallucination or whatever it was, found himself walking in silence towards the canteen with Katherine by his side. Silently thanking his gran for insisting he never leave the house without some nanny-money (money you take 'just in case', but never usually spend), he ordered two coffees. It was a typical hospital canteen with a counter down one side where you help yourself to whatever food or cold drinks you want and then, at the very end where they take the money, was the hot drinks counter. The room was quite large, but sparsely furnished with cheap plastic chairs and square tables, most of which wobbled on uneven legs when touched. They were the only people there apart from the woman behind the counter who looked very bored. When the coffees arrived they chose a table at the far end of the room near a large window.

'So, everything go okay with the doc?' Katherine asked.

'Er, yeah, thanks,' Jack replied. 'You?'

'Oh, I didn't have an appointment,' she explained, 'I was just visiting my uncle.'

'Your uncle?' Jack repeated, a bit stupidly.

'Yes, Dr Noah, he's my uncle, didn't you know?'

'No,' replied Jack.

'Oh,' she said a little surprised, 'I thought you might have guessed after we came to your grandparents' Christmas party together.'

'What? Oh, yeah, right,' said Jack, of course he was her uncle, why had he not realised that before?

They chatted for a while about Dr Noah and the party, both of them avoiding mentioning the part where he dropped his drink and ran upstairs. They briefly touched on school and which teachers and subjects they liked and disliked. Jack mentioned Eric and was pleased to see Katherine's face contort into a grimace as she started ranting about how much she disliked him.

'He's awful,' she said, 'he thinks he's God's gift when really he's just an idiotic bully.'

Jack's insides sang at her words.

'He kept asking me out when I first came to the school,' she went on, 'as if. No way, never!'

Jack laughed. 'I don't like him much either,' he said.

'I bet you don't,' she replied 'I've heard the way he speaks to you... and your friend, Dennis, is it? He's just a horrible person and that awful gang of his... I mean, have you ever smelled that dreadful Matt boy, he reeks.'

They both laughed and carried on abusing Eric and his friends for a bit longer.

'Why did you move to our school?' Jack asked her. 'I heard you moved here from somewhere abroad?'

'Er, well, yes,' she stammered, 'my parents live in, er, France. They decided it would be better if I lived with my uncle for a while and came back to school in England. I've got to admit, it was a good move. I do prefer the company,' she said, smiling.

Jack blushed, hoping she was talking about him.

They chatted some more; she told him she was an only child and, when he asked, she confirmed she had no pets.

'I love animals,' he had said, 'my gran won't let me have any, but when I get a place of my own I'll fill it with pets.'

'I don't like animals kept in captivity,' she had explained.

'Captivity?' he had been surprised at her choice of words, 'surely cats and dogs are okay, I mean, they aren't kept in cages or anything.'

'They're still not free though, are they?' she asked, 'they can't just go where they want, when they want.'

'Well, no, I s'pose dogs can't but surely cats are pretty free?' he'd asked, 'they go wherever they want, we have one that comes in our garden a lot, no one makes her.'

He explained all about Poppy.

She looked at him thoughtfully and then smiled.

There was a slight lull in the conversation; Jack decided now was the time to go for it.

'Katherine, can I ask you something, something personal? You can say no, obviously.' The last bit he added quickly, looking embarrassed.

'Okay, but only if you call me Kat,' she said playfully.

'Okay, Kat,' he said. 'Can I ask you something?'

'Of course,' she said, smiling.

'Have you ever had a heart transplant?'

'What?' she asked half confused, half laughing; whatever she had expected him to ask it was obviously not this.

'A heart transplant, have you ever had one?' he repeated going red again, 'or any sort of heart surgery, really,' he added quickly.

'No,' she said, still looking confused. 'Why would you ask that?'

Jack bit his lip. *Now or never,* he thought.

'Well it's just… your arm, the, you know, disc-thing… like I have.' And he held up his left wrist and pulled back his sweatband to show her.

She looked at his wrist and then down at her own.

'Oh,' she said, quietly going red. Then, looking at the other side of her wrist, she glanced her watch and announced.

'Sorry, Jack, I've got to go, sorry… bye,' and with that she got up from the table and practically ran from the canteen.

Jack just sat watching the door she had disappeared through; he felt terrible, why had he just blurted it out like that? Why had he not waited, waited until he knew her better or until the moment had been better or something, anything but on their first real meeting. His insides that had been so happy a moment ago, now felt as though they had sunk into his feet and he felt a bit sick. If only he could turn the clock back.

Sighing to himself, he got up from the table and slowly walked to the door. *Might as well go get that bus home*, he thought to himself. As he walked outside, he blinked a bit in the bright sunshine; it was one of those bright but cold days. He pulled his jacket tighter around his body and started towards home.

'Jack.' He heard a small voice call him.

He spun round and saw Katherine standing right behind him.

'Sorry,' they both said together.

'No, I'm sorry,' said Jack, 'I shouldn't have said anything. I'm such an idiot.'

'No, I'm sorry,' Katherine said, 'I overreacted. You asked a perfectly polite question and I stormed out on you.'

'Can we just forget I asked, please?' Jack begged.

She looked at him.

'No,' she said sadly, 'I can't forget it, but neither can I answer it, can we just leave it for now and I will tell you all about it when I can?'

'Okay,' said Jack, 'fine… can I still call you Kat?' he added to try to break the awkwardness.

She laughed, 'Of course.'

'Can I walk you home?' Jack offered hopefully.

She looked at him thoughtfully.

'Yes,' she said, 'I'd like that.'

They set off walking in silence, it did not feel awkward to Jack; in fact, it felt quite comfortable. They walked through streets and a park until eventually Katherine said.

'Well this is me,' and she pointed at an old, large house whose walls were covered in ivy. Jack, who had not been taking much notice where he was walking to was surprised to find himself in a very nice part of town, typical doctor's house he had found himself thinking, nice. They said goodbye and as she was walking up the driveway Jack called after her.

'Kat, would you like to go out with me on Saturday?' *Please*, he added silently.

'Yes,' she replied, and ran back down the drive to give him her mobile number.

Saturday arrived to find Jack a bundle of nerves; what on earth were they going to do today? They had arranged to meet at one o'clock in the afternoon, but that was as far as the plans went at the moment. As soon as the time reached past nine in the morning, Jack was on the phone to Dennis.

'Help me, Den!' he had almost shouted down the phone. 'What am I going to do?'

'With what?' Dennis had replied sleepily.

'With Katherine, today. Where can I take her? What can we do?'

Dennis had taken a few minutes to properly wake up.

'Okay,' he had said at last, 'how about going to see a film? That way you don't have to think of something to say, then afterwards you can go somewhere like McDonalds and if the conversation gets difficult you can always talk about the film.'

'You're a genius,' said Jack. 'That's brilliant, what's on at the flicks, do you know?'

'At the what, mate?' Dennis asked, laughing.

Jack could feel his face getting hot and was glad he was on the phone and Dennis could not see him.

'Sorry,' Jack said. 'Bad habit, my gran always calls it the flicks.'

'You might want to break that habit before you say it to Katherine, not very hip, mate.' Dennis said, still laughing.

They had spent the next few minutes discussing the different films on offer at the local cinema and eventually decided a romantic comedy was probably the best option, even though Jack would have preferred something with a bit of action. He had never even heard of the movie they chose, but Jack decided it would not matter because he doubted he would be able to concentrate with Katherine sitting next to him anyway.

At midday Jack set off to get the bus into town, Pam had offered to drive him, but he had declined, thinking it would make him feel better if he went under his own steam. He got to Katherine's house far too early, so hung around outside for at least fifteen minutes so she would not think he was too keen. At ten to one he knocked on the door, hoping Katherine would answer. He was slightly alarmed when the door opened and Dr Noah appeared on the other side, but the doctor smiled and invited Jack to come and wait inside.

'Katherine, Jackson is here,' Dr Noah called up the stairs. Turning to Jack, he added, 'Please, Jackson, take a seat in the living room,' and he pointed to a door on the left. Jack went into the room; it was large and airy with patio doors opening onto a large and well-kept garden, although it was quite sparse this time of year. There were two large, old-looking leather settees with lots of cushions and a coffee table with a large vase of fresh flowers. Jack found himself wondering whether there was a Mrs Noah; the cushions and the flowers had a female feel to them. Just then, Katherine entered the room, smiling, she said, 'Hi, Jack.'

'Hi,' he replied blushing, he really wished he would not do that.

'So what do you want to do?' she asked. 'Something indoors, I hope, it's freezing out there,' she added, laughing.

'I thought perhaps the cinema,' Jack offered, 'there's a, er, comedy on,' he had not wanted to say *romantic*. '*To the Moon and Back*, I think it's called.'

'Okay,' Katherine said, 'sounds nice and warm, let's give it a go.'

The movie had not been great; not particularly funny and rather too much kissing for Jack to have felt particularly comfortable, but sitting next to Katherine in the dark, sharing a large box of sweet popcorn had gone a long way to make up for what the film lacked. Walking out of the cinema, Jack turned to Katherine and asked, 'Are you hungry? There's a McDonalds just down the road.'

'Okay, I am a bit hungry,' she replied.

They walked to McDonalds in silence, both wrapped up warm against the cold air, which seemed to have got even colder since they went in the cinema and now the light was fading. The restaurant as very bright and warm, Katherine found a table by the window and Jack ordered two Big Mac meals with Coke and brought them over to the table. They ate and chatted easily, they talked briefly about the film, but neither of them had liked it much so they discussed what they did like.

'I don't watch many movies,' Katherine admitted, 'I don't watch much TV either.'

'I love TV,' Jack said enthusiastically, 'I love anything about animals, wildlife documentaries in particular. I love lions and tigers the best.'

'I love the big cats too,' Katherine agreed, 'I love all animals though, big or small.'

'Me too,' Jack enthused. 'When I leave school, I want to work with animals.'

'Doing what?' Katherine asked.

'Dunno, anything,' Jack said.

They finished their food and Jack walked Katherine home. When they got to her house, she turned to him and went to kiss him on the cheek; Jack had got flustered when he had seen her moving closer to him and had moved at just the wrong moment and the kiss had found his lips instead. They kissed briefly, both surprised, then Katherine pulled away.

'I like you Jack. I like you a lot,' she said in a small voice.

Jack's heart was pounding. *Can't be good for it*, he briefly thought. He was sure his voice would not work properly.

'I like you too,' he squeaked.

She smiled and then turned and ran inside her house. Jack

walked towards the bus stop on air; she liked him, she liked him a lot. He felt like skipping.

Their second date to the bowling alley was a great success. Jack had wanted to go to the zoo, but Katherine reminded him of her feelings about animals in captivity.

'Are you mad?' she had asked him in a stern voice, 'I can't stand animals in cages, I thought you knew me?'

'Sorry, I forgot, it was just my favourite place when I was younger...' Jack trailed off, hoping she would forgive him quickly.

She did.

The bowling alley had been Katherine's idea and had been great fun. Jack, as it turned out, was quite good at bowling and had beaten Katherine easily.

Their third date was not quite so exciting; Jack went to Katherine's house to do homework with her. The prospect of doing homework was never very appealing to Jack, but somehow being with Katherine made it a lot more fun. She had a way of explaining things that made them interesting and she was funny and cute. Over the next couple of weeks, Jack and Katherine became inseparable; every spare minute at school, and as much time at the weekends as possible, they were together. Doing homework, going for walks, eating burgers, whatever they did, they did together. Jack was so happy he thought he might burst. Katherine was everything he had imagined her to be: funny, caring and clever. He was even starting to feel at home when he went to her house; Dr Noah was very discreet and would usually find some work that needed doing somewhere else in the house whenever they were in the lounge. Jack discovered there was no Mrs Noah, though there had been. Dr Noah had married very young, but unfortunately Mrs Noah had died a long time ago, though no one had said what of. The feminine touches in the house were all down to Katherine and their housekeeper Mrs Tumble, a widow in her sixties who loved to bake cakes and cookies and force Katherine and Jack to eat them, which they certainly never objected to.

Katherine was a welcome visitor at Jack's house too; Pam and Alan loved her, she was so polite and helpful and, as far as they were concerned, anyone who made Jack that happy was okay with them. Jack was careful not to neglect Dennis and made sure he made time for his friend and invited him along with him and Katherine whenever it was appropriate. Katherine and Dennis really got on, which was a relief for Jack. However close they got though, Jack never asked about the wrist-disc-thing again and Katherine never volunteered any information.

Jack was dreaming again; he was running, running very fast. No, not running exactly, more like galloping, though not exactly galloping either. He was definitely running on all fours, which when he realised, seemed weird, but had not up until then. He was also barefoot again. He was again, running through a town, past shops and bus stops and cars, but no people. There was not anyone around and it was dark. He reached the edge of the town and started running through grassland, it was very dark, but it did not bother him, he could see perfectly. He was completely focussed on his goal, though he could not remember exactly what it was, he knew it had something to do with the wrist-disc and Katherine. He knew there was no time to waste. Running past a lake, he realised his throat was dry and so stopped for a quick drink. Catching his reflection in the lakes surface by the moonlight, he was shocked to see a large shaggy head looking back at him; a large, shaggy head that resembled a large, shaggy dog more than a human boy. Jack awoke sweating. Lying in his room in the dark, he felt his face; it felt normal, though Jack was not sure he even knew what normal was anymore.

Jack's seventeenth birthday arrived on a cold snowy day. After a long walk in the snow with Katherine where they made a snowman, or actually, to be more precise, they made a slightly lop-sided snow-bear. They stopped by a frozen lake and watched the ducks slipping around on the ice. Katherine gave Jack a small wrapped package.

'Happy birthday, Jack,' she said, 'it's just a small thing, I thought you might like it.'

Jack pulled the paper off and found a paperback book about British wildlife and a key ring with a metal tiger on it.

'Thanks,' Jack said, genuinely pleased, 'I love them both.' And he kissed her.

When the light started to fade they made their way back to Jack's house, where Pam greeted them with hot chocolate and they warmed their frozen red faces by the fire. Dennis arrived at about five o'clock with a huge tin of chocolate from his Mum and Dad and a new game for the Wii from him. At seven o'clock Pam and Alan took them all to a posh restaurant just outside of town. Jack noticed the menu did not have any prices on it, which was sure to mean they were very high. They all ate expensive smoked salmon and king prawns and ridiculously overpriced steaks and finished by stuffing themselves with death-by-chocolate until they all felt sick. It was a wonderful evening.

That evening, when Jack was getting ready for bed, he was so happy he did not notice at first when the pain started. It started in his knees and travelled down to his feet, when he looked down he could see his toenails were twisting and turning and sort of moulding together into what looked like claws. The pain was incredible and it took all of Jack's strength not to cry out. He watched as his feet started to shrink and his toes bend under on themselves. He fell to the floor panting, but just as suddenly as it had started, it stopped; the pain and the hallucination or whatever it was. He carefully got to his feet and went into his bathroom, he sat down on the side of the bath, thinking hard about all the things that had and were happening to him: the strength, the energy, the healthy look, the dreams and the… what? Because they certainly were not hallucinations, whatever they were, they were very real. Jack looked at his face in the mirror. If the things that were happening were real then something was making them happen. What though? What on earth could possibly be doing this to him? He thought back to each situation. The stump on the base of his spine; that had been the morning after the Christmas party. What had been unusual about that morning? He thought about it; nothing really, he had been happy, he had woken up happy, nothing strange about that. The hair on his hands had happened when he had been introduced to Katherine. Now, that had been a strange situation; wanting to meet her for ages and then finding her in his house, he had felt excited and a little nervous to be finally meeting her, he remembered thinking he was bound to stutter or something. The leg; that had happened after he had fallen off the bike; he had been bleeding and a bit embarrassed, but he had also felt angry, angry at himself for losing control. And just now, the feet thing, he had just had a lovely evening with his family and best friends and he was happy, really happy. So the only common thing between all these events was that he had been either happy or angry or something, was it feelings or something related to how he was feeling? Emotions perhaps, could they be the key? If he felt particularly emotional did this trigger the strange events? And if emotions could cause these things to happen and control what happened to him, was there a way he himself could turn things around and control them? He was still staring in the mirror, what if he imagined something happening to his face. He thought really hard, imagining his face covered in hair, he screwed up his eyes and held his breath, concentrating. Nothing happened. He tried to think of something else. He imagined his ears growing bigger, imagined it as hard as he could, but still nothing happened. Perhaps he needed to concentrate on recreating something that had already happened. The stump, he thought hard about that, trying to imagine how it would feel if something was growing out of his skin. Still nothing. He felt foolish and embarrassed, even though he was alone. What had he been thinking? He got up and moved to the wash basin to clean his teeth, as he opened his mouth he gasped – his teeth, they were all pointy, like a mouth full of vampire teeth. Instead of panicking like he had before, he tried to remain calm. He looked at his teeth – *his teeth?* The teeth in his mouth anyway. He had always been quite proud of his teeth, straight and white and strong. These teeth were a long way from straight and white, they were yellowy and pointy and looked as though they would be good at tearing meat from a bone and, actually, they looked as though they would be good at splintering bones as well. He moved his head from side to side, studying them from every angle, weird. He looked down into the basin, turned on the cold tap and splashed his face with cold water. As he suspected, when he looked up, his teeth were back to normal.

Jack thought about the 'changes', as he now preferred to think of them, a lot over the next few days. Whenever he was alone at home, which was not very often, he would try to make something happen, but he was unable to make so much as a hair grow. What he really wanted was to discuss all the weird stuff with someone, get it off his chest, see if someone else could make any sense of it, but who could he talk to? He did not want to bother his grandparents, they were so happy now Jack was fit and healthy, and they had suffered through so many years of worry over him that he did not want to add to that. He could not talk to Dennis, he did not think Dennis would understand, besides, he was very busy with his driving lessons; having already passed his theory test, he was working hard towards the practical. That only left Dr Noah. Jack did not find the doctor very easy to talk to, he made Jack feel uneasy, as he had always had the feeling that Dr Noah knew something he was not letting on, something about Jack. Still, Jack made an appointment to see him in a couple of weeks, telling himself he would see how things went and decide on the day just how much he would divulge. The funny thing was, whenever Jack thought about discussing these things, it was always Katherine's face he saw in his mind, Katherine who was always so understanding, Katherine who always had an answer for everything, Katherine who would probably run a mile if he ever mentioned what was happening to him. *Best to leave that well alone*, he thought with a shiver.

But Jack never went to the appointment he made with Dr Noah; two days after making it, Jack's granddad had a massive heart attack and died almost instantly.

5.

STARTING AGAIN

The sky was grey and the sleet was getting heavier, the wind was blowing and all the people were walking with their heads bent down and their arms huddled around themselves trying to stay dry and warm. Although it was only two in the afternoon, it was already nearly dark on that horrible February day. Pam was crying, she was bent over the side of the grave, so far into her grief she was barely aware anyone else was around. Most of the other mourners had left or were leaving, except Pam at the graveside and Katherine who was standing behind Jack. Jack stood looking at his grandmother, neither knowing nor caring that he was soaked through to the skin and shivering. The last few days had been something of a blur for Jack. The phone call had said that Alan had had a heart attack while playing golf with some friends and Jack and Pam had rushed to the hospital, only to find Alan had not made it that far, he had died in the ambulance on the way. The fact that he had already had a mild attack two years before had come as a complete shock to both Pam and Jack who had never known anything about it. Pam was distraught; the only man she had ever loved, taken from her so cruelly. Jack too had been devastated, the man who had raised him, taught him and loved him, one of only two people who had always been there for him – people he had thought would always be there for him – suddenly gone, and he never even got to say goodbye. He had tried so hard to be strong for his gran, the last thing she needed was him crying and moping but when he was alone in his room he could not hold it in anymore.

He guessed it was because his emotions were all over the place that the changes started happening daily and sometimes more than once a day. At first they only added to his grief, making him resentful and angry, as if he did not have enough to worry about and, obviously, that made them worse. But after a while they started becoming an almost welcome distraction, taking his mind off his misery if only for a few seconds. The first time he had changed after Alan had died had been very traumatic; Jack had been overcome with grief and had given into crying, thankfully alone in his room, lying face down on his bed. The pain had been sudden and sharp, hitting him completely off guard. He had cried out as the stabbing pain shot through both his legs, up and down. He had sat up and tried to watch as the bones contracted and became thinner and longer, he had called out again when his skin and muscles and fat had felt like they were being torn to shreds by something with large teeth. This pain and the stretching and ripping went on for a few minutes, completely exhausting him. Once it started to subside he just had time to catch his breath before it started again, only this time on his arms. Jack had been terrified; he was lying on his bed unable to get up because the form his legs and arms had taken on were not strong enough to hold up his still human body. He lay there for a while, panicking that his gran could walk in at any moment. After a few minutes he reasoned that panicking was not going to help; on the contrary, it would probably make things worse. He tried to calm himself down; he took several long, deep breaths and told himself that this would not last forever. He needed to control this thing instead of it controlling him. He had sat up and, still breathing deeply, had used the soft under part of his hands – no, his *paws* – to rub his temples. Slowly, he could feel his heart rate slowing and his breathing easing and he had continued this way until he felt, well not completely calm but calm enough to think clearly. Slowly and calmly he concentrated on one leg at a time and then one arm at a time until he willed his usual human limbs to return. Then he relaxed.

Four days later he had experienced nearly every part of his body change somehow, at different times. Mostly it was fur growing all over him, including his face, but it was also body parts changing shape; still remaining recognisable as a leg or arm, but most definitely not human. These changes would have been fascinating if they had not been so very painful. The hair growing was not painful, that felt strange, a sort of mixture between a tickling and a prickling sensation, not exactly nice, but not totally unpleasant either. No, it was the shape changing that hurt, he could actually feel, (and hear) his bones stretching or becoming smaller and pulling muscle and fat and skin with them. The pain sometimes made him cry out loud. Despite the pain and the fact that he was terrified, Jack did not want the changes to stop, although he had no idea what was wrong with him and why he should be experiencing such weird things. So far the changes had been limited so that only parts of him changed at any one time. Jack could feel it was only a matter of time before they started happening at the same time and then his whole body would change, change into what though? The changes did not last long, he would watch as his fingers would retract into his hands, leaving short stumps that sort of resembled paws and then watched as gnarled, knobbly things would grow out the ends, he guessed these were claws. And a few seconds later he would watch as they would all disappear again and his fingers would reappear. Jack knew he should be more concerned by these changes and what they meant, he knew he should be trying to find out what was happening to him and why, he should be talking to Dr Noah in the hope he might have some answers, although really was anyone likely to have answers to these questions? And if he did speak to Dr Noah, what would he say?

'*Hey, Doc, I seem to be turning into some sort of animal when I get emotional, what can you tell me about that?*' Even inside his head it sounded ridiculous.

Despite the pain and the fear, the things he was going through somehow felt very personal to him and now that he was starting to get used to it he just was not ready to share it yet. Besides, he did not want to be locked away for his own safety; he had not ruled out that he was losing his mind.

Jack looked over at the old grave next to his granddad's fresh one, it was the usual shield-shaped stone covered in moss, but was still recognisable. The stone read:

'*Sharon Anne King, 1974 – 1992, Much loved Daughter and Mother, Never Forgotten.*'

His mother. He wondered what she would be doing if she was here now. What she would say? Would she be comforting him or would she have been so consumed in her own grief that she could not spare a thought for him? He wondered what she had been like, what sort of mother she would have been, what his life would have been like had she not been killed. Would she know what was happening to him? Would she have been able to answer his questions? One thing he did know, she was the only person who knew who his father was, the only person who could have told him and his father, who, Jack was sure was as much in the dark as he was, about each other. She had literally taken that bit of information to the grave with her.

Katherine took Jack's hand in hers and they both crossed over to where Pam was weeping.

'Gran,' he whispered gently, 'it's time to go.'

She looked up at him, her once pretty face was streaked with tears and a small sob escaped her lips. Jack took her arm and helped her straighten up. She looked so small, standing there crying. She had always been so strong, so dependable, now Jack would have to be the strong one; it was his turn to look after her.

They went back to the house, everyone had been invited back for drinks and Pam had spent the last couple of days in the kitchen preparing a spread any royal house would be proud of. Some people were already waiting for them when they arrived. Jack opened the door and let everyone inside, expecting Pam to still be unable to cope. He was surprised when she shook herself down and pushed past him into the house to take her place as the hostess. Jack felt a huge rush of love for his gran. Even at her lowest moment she put on a brave face and tried to carry on as normal; he could not help but admire her resolve, he himself felt like curling into a ball and crying, but if Gran could be brave then so could he. The wake did not last long, most people only stayed a couple of hours and then left. By five o'clock in the afternoon there was only Pam, Jack, Katherine, Dennis and Dennis' parents left. Dennis' parents had not known Alan very well; they had only met a couple of times, but had insisted on attending the funeral to support Jack. Now Mr and Mrs Gribben stood at the kitchen sink washing the last of the glasses while the others sat around the island in the kitchen, no one speaking, all deep in thought. Jack thought Pam looked exhausted, she had coped so well today, but it had taken it out of her. Tomorrow she was leaving to go and stay with an old friend who lived down on the south coast for a couple of weeks. Everyone had agreed the change of scene and the sea air would do her good. She had been worried about leaving Jack alone, but he had insisted he would be fine.

'Go,' he had told her, 'please go, it will do you good. Don't worry about me, I'll be fine, I've got Kat and I can ask Den to come and stay.'

But he would not ask Dennis to come and stay, he wanted some time on his own, he wanted some time to experiment.

'Come on, Dennis,' Mrs Gribben had said, hanging up the tea towel. 'Time we were making a move, leave these people in peace.'

They had all got up and the Gribben's had left, leaving Jack, Katherine and Pam alone. They hugged each other and then, although it was still very early, Pam said she was ready for bed. Jack knew she had not been sleeping well, he had heard her in the middle of the night crying when she thought he was asleep.

'Night, Gran,' he whispered, 'sleep well.'

'Night, sweetie,' she replied, 'love you.'

Jack and Katherine sat for a long time in the kitchen, not speaking, just holding hands, until eventually Dr Noah arrived to give Katherine a lift home.

Jack stared at his reflection; he moved his head from side to side to get a better look from every angle. He was not sure what he was, though he thought this time he definitely had canine characteristics, though that was not always so. He was not fully whatever the animal was, he was sort of half and half. His torso was still human, though covered in fur. His arms were human, but thinner and he no longer had hands, he had what he supposed must be paws. The same for his legs, they were still human, but his feet had been replaced with the same sort of paws, that were not quite holding up his still quite thick legs, so he was sitting on the toilet seat. He definitely had a snout of some sort and his teeth were very pointy. Jack was not keen on the feel of his teeth when they were like this, he felt like he could easily cut his tongue, and was therefore very careful. He had the very painful stump at the base of his spine, he had not managed what he assumed would eventually be a full tail as yet, and was not planning to – the growing process was excruciating and he always got so far and then tried to halt it. Since he'd had the house to himself for the last week he had practised and practised gaining control of this changing thing and was definitely improving. He could now make fur grow anywhere he wanted almost every time; he had chosen fur to practice with because it was the least painful. He had discovered that changing a body part from human to whatever it was he was changing to was very painful, he could feel every part of him stretching or retracting and this caused a lot of pain, not as much pain, however, as growing a new body part. Growing something new, for example a tail, was the worst pain, it felt like his flesh was being ripped apart. So far he had only got as far as the stump, but not only was the growing painful, but the actual stump itself was so incredibly tender that Jack could not bear to touch it and he had therefore decided this should be avoided at all cost. Of all the changes to all the parts of his body he had managed to make, his eyes were the one thing he could not make change at all. He had concentrated really hard on making them change from their usual brown to green or blue. He had tried making them change to slit pupils instead of the usual round ones, but no luck, they just stayed completely the same. Jack found this frustrating because this was the one change he could explain easily to others if it happened in company – colour-change lenses!

One evening, while Pam was still away at her friend's house and a rare occasion when Jack was not seeing Katherine, Jack asked Dennis round for a few beers and a takeaway. They were sitting back on the settees, sipping lager and uncomfortably full from eating too much curry, when Jack decided the time had come to let Dennis in on his new secret.

'I'm leaving school,' he announced, 'I haven't told gran yet, but it just doesn't make sense to stay on. I mean, I'm rubbish. I've never been good at it and I think it would be best if I got a job.'

Dennis stared at him.

'Blimey,' he said. 'What sort of job?'

'Dunno,' Jack replied. 'Something working with animals would be good though.'

He had been thinking about this for a long time. Jack loved animals; they had never had any pets when he was younger because Pam was too house-proud. He had seen a sign at the local animal shelter for a general helper. The pay was terrible, but Jack did not need the money, his granddad had left both him and his gran very well off, so he had applied and was waiting to hear back.

Dennis was thoughtful for a while, he had never been very good at school either, but Mr and Mrs Gribben had insisted he stay on at school and at least try.

'Wish I could leave school,' he said grumpily, 'I'm rubbish too. As soon as I pass my driving test I'm going to talk to Mum and Dad again about letting me leave. I want to earn money.'

Having already failed his practical driving test twice, Jack doubted that would be anytime soon.

Jack would not miss school.

When Pam came home after nearly three weeks away she looked much better. Her face did not look so drawn and she looked as though she had gained a little weight. She was also a lot brighter in herself.

'We can't mope around all the time,' she had told Jack. 'Your granddad wouldn't want us to be sad, he would be cross with us for wasting valuable time grieving.'

Jack had told her of his plans for leaving school and starting work, he had been offered the position at the animal shelter and was just awaiting Pam's approval before accepting. She had looked at him and smiled, he smiled back waiting for the onslaught, he was ready for a fight.

'My little boy,' she had said, 'all grown up.' She had looked a little sad, but then she added, 'If that's what you want, sweetie. If your granddad has shown us anything, it's that we shouldn't waste time doing things we don't want to. Yes, if that's what you want, then you go for it.'

He was a little surprised he did not have to defend his decision, but very glad. He hugged her and kissed her cheek.

A few days later, Jack was starting work. He arrived at eight o'clock in the morning. The moment he got within a few yards of the gate the overwhelming animal smells hit him like something physical; there were so many all mixed together it was quite confusing. Taking some deep breaths through his mouth, Jack tried sniffing gently and was not totally surprised when the smells starting coming to him separately, although he was not sure which animal each smell came from, he could tell the different ones apart. He was greeted by a slight, pretty and quite lively young woman in her early twenties. She was wearing dirty green overalls and pink wellington boots and her long dark brown hair was pulled back into a scraggy ponytail. She smiled as she said hello.

'Hi, I'm Nora. You must be Jack. I'm going to show you around and explain how things work,' she explained, holding her hand out to Jack.

Jack shook her hand.

'Hi,' he said, feeling slightly awkward.

'We need to get you into some overalls and wellingtons,' she added thoughtfully. 'It can get pretty mucky round here.'

She started walking towards the main house and Jack followed.

The house was large and set in its own grounds. Jack looked around and thought it may once have been quite grand with a long sweeping drive and carefully manicured lawns, now, however, it was run-down and there was evidence of animals all over the place, from the chickens pecking at the ground, to the rabbits in long runs nibbling at the overgrown grass, to buckets of feed and wheelbarrows of manure that littered the gravel drive. Nora noticed him looking around.

'Pretty messy, huh?' she asked. 'We have so many animals we just can't keep it tidy, besides, the animals don't mind. As long as they have food and somewhere to sleep and a bit of love, that's all they really care about,' she said, smiling.

They went inside the main door into a large hallway that was obviously used as part dumping ground, part storage room. It was completely littered with shoes, feed, wellingtons, coats and all manner of other stuff. Boxes were piled up against the walls, bags that were over-spilling were shoved into corners and two bikes were propped up by the door. Nora started rummaging around in a large cupboard on the left-hand side of the room; she turned over several old jumpers and coats until she found what she was looking for.

'These look like they might fit,' she said, holding out some old, but clean looking navy overalls to Jack. He took them and started pulling them on over his jeans.

'What size shoes do you take?' she asked.

'Ten,' he replied. Since the operation and the increase in his weight, he had found his feet had grown in size from an eight to a ten; he hoped they were not going to get any bigger, he was tired of buying new shoes.

Nora bent down and was going through a box on the floor of the cupboard. She pulled out a pair of green wellington boots and handed them to him.

'Try these, I think they're an eleven, but they might be okay until we can find a better pair,' she said.

Jack removed his trainers and pulled the boots on, they were a bit big, but would do; he made a mental note to bring extra pair of socks tomorrow. Nora stood up.

'Okay, now you're all kitted out, let's go look around.' And she headed back out the door.

Jack followed her. They walked across the front of the house and around the side where they went through a tall gate. On the other side of the gate was a large open area, which Jack assumed would have been the garden in the days when the house was just a house. Now though, there was not much grass, most of it had been replaced with concrete. All around the edges were outhouses and stables. Nora led him towards the first building and pushed the door open. Inside were several large cages housing small animals: rabbits, squirrels, a fox and several polecats. They all looked warily towards the door and the extra light. It was warm and stuffy inside the shed and very smelly.

'Injured wildlife,' Nora explained, 'usually nothing bigger than a fox or two, but occasionally we get the odd badger.'

She walked back outside and waited for Jack to come out before closing the door. They headed to the next door; again it contained several large cages, this time housing cats. Each door led to a different room that held a different species of animal or bird, and finally, the stables, which had sheep, goats, two horses, a pony and a donkey.

'All the animals here have been injured, abandoned or abused. My dad is a vet and he has his own practice so he can treat all those that need it. Some stay here a long time because it's hard to re-house them. Some, like the squirrels and foxes and the birds, we release as soon as they are fit and well,' Nora explained. 'What we need you to do is feed the animals and keep them clean. The dogs need walking and the bigger animals, like the horses and sheep and goats, need to be let out to graze, it's easy.' She smiled.

At the end of Jack's first week of working at the animal centre, he was absolutely exhausted. He had fed, cleaned, walked, tidied, fed more, cleaned more, walked more and so on, it was never ending. Despite the aching back, the blisters that the too big wellington boots had rubbed on his feet and the utter exhaustion, Jack had loved his first week. He now knew all the animals by name and by their smell; he did not have to see them to know which breed and, indeed, which individual was nearest him. It had become very obvious very quickly that the animals liked Jack, they seemed to trust him and they also seemed to listen to him, coming if he called them. It was also obvious that Jack liked the animals; this was not only obvious to the animals, but also to Nora who had stopped what she was doing on several occasions to watch Jack and marvel at the way he had with all the animals.

'You're a natural,' she had said to him on the last day of his first week, 'the animals trust you and you trust them, you're very lucky.'

They were sitting under a tree eating sandwiches and drinking Coke, enjoying the unusually warm April sunshine.

'I've always liked animals,' Jack admitted, swinging his Coke bottle back and forth. 'They're so much easier to get on with than people, they don't judge you because of what you look like. As long as you're kind to them they're usually kind back.'

'You're right,' Nora said, 'but even so, most people don't get the sort of response you get, most people have to work hard to gain an animal's trust, especially wild animals, but they just trust you, they like you, it's almost as if they see you as one of them.'

Jack had not said anything but chewed his food thoughtfully. The front gate had opened at that point and a young dark haired girl had walked in.

'Jack, meet my little sister, Bryony,' Nora had said.

Jack looked up and saw Bryony, the girl from school that Dennis was still very keen on but still had not found the courage to ask out.

'Hi,' he said.

She blushed.

'Hi,' she whispered. 'You're Dennis' friend, aren't you?'

'I'm telling you, Den, let me set it up, me and Kat and you and Bryony,' Jack was on the phone to Dennis. 'She mentioned you straight away, why would she do that if she wasn't interested. She knew I was your friend.'

Dennis was silent.

'Den?' Jack asked, 'you still there?'

'Yeah, just thinking, mate, hang on.'

'What's there to think about? You've liked her for ages.' Jack couldn't believe Dennis was being like this, he had been sure Dennis would have jumped at the chance. Still there was silence on the other end of the phone.

'Den?' Jack asked again.

'Yeah, yeah, I'm here,' Dennis replied eventually. 'Look, mate, I appreciate you trying to help and all that, but I'm too busy at the moment, so I think I'll have to say no.'

'WHAT?' Jack almost shouted, 'What do you mean you're too busy, too busy doing what?'

'You know, school work, trying to pass my driving test...' Dennis trailed off.

'And you can't spare a couple of hours for a date with the girl you've liked for ages?' Jack asked sarcastically.

'No,' Dennis said bluntly, 'I can't.'

No matter how Jack tried to persuade Dennis he just would not budge. After a few more minutes talking, realising he was fighting a losing battle, Jack said goodbye and hung up, still shocked at his friend's response. What could possibly be wrong with Dennis that was making him act so strangely?

There was nothing else for it, Jack would have to go round and see Dennis in person.

Jack arrived at Dennis' house thirty minutes later; he had stopped at a petrol station to buy crisps and chocolate, knowing these would soften Dennis up a bit. Dennis opened the door and was shocked to see Jack standing there, though not as shocked as Jack was to see Dennis. Dennis' face was covered in tiny cuts and marks; he looked as though he had been fighting with a cat with very sharp claws. Dennis moved back to allow Jack to enter the house. Once they were in the lounge, Jack turned to Dennis and asked him what had happened to his face.

Dennis looked embarrassed, 'I can't get the hang of it,' Dennis moaned, 'all these changes, I can't get used to it at all.'

Jack froze, what changes was Dennis talking about? He could not possibly be going through the same things as Jack could he? Jack's heart started racing as he looked into Dennis' eyes and asked.

'What changes, Den? What can't you get the hang of?'

He waited, hardly breathing, for Dennis' reply; it would be so great to have someone to share all this madness with. Dennis looked even more embarrassed.

'Can't you tell from my face?' he asked, 'I would have thought it was pretty obvious.'

'No,' whispered Jack, 'what?'

'Shaving,' Dennis said in a small voice, 'I can't get the hang of shaving. I just keep cutting myself all the time.'

'Shaving?' Jack said stupidly, 'Oh, shaving,' he said, realisation dawning and his heartbeat returning to normal.

It was as much as Jack could do not to laugh, although disappointment flooded through him at the thought that Dennis was not about to reveal the answers to all Jack's questions, but he was relieved that Dennis' problem was as trivial as shaving.

'Is this why you won't go out with Bryony? Jack asked, 'because you keep cutting your face shaving?'

'Yes,' Dennis admitted miserably.

Again Jack wanted to laugh but stopped himself.

'Hey, don't be silly, Den, practice makes perfect, we could have a great night out and maybe it could be the start of you and Bryony. Don't ruin it just because you've cut your face a bit.' Jack bit his lip, waiting for Dennis to reply.

Dennis laughed.

'I'm an idiot, aren't I?' He said sheepishly, 'yeah, guess you should have a go at setting up a date, thanks mate.'

6.

THE ATTACK

'Who would like a drink?' Jack asked.

The four of them were sitting in the lounge at Jack's house, they had just got back from the bowling alley and were quite tired and in need of something to drink. This was the third date the four of them had been on together. The first one had gone very well, Katherine and Bryony had hit it off straight away, they were both quite shy and quiet and shared a love of animals. Dennis had made a special effort to look his best; he had abandoned his traditional jeans and t-shirt for a smart shirt and trousers and had even put gel in his hair to make it look stylishly tousled. He had got over his issues with shaving a few days before, when Jack had suggested he buy an electric razor instead of wet shaving, this had proved very successful and, by the time the date came around, the cuts on Dennis' face had almost all disappeared. That first evening they had gone to the cinema and endured nearly two hours of a truly dreadful film called *The Straight Man,* this had definitely broken the ice, though, when they had gone for a MacDonald's afterwards and spent the next hour laughing and tearing the movie apart. Tonight, however, now that he felt more comfortable in Bryony's company, Dennis was back in his casual attire.

'I'd love a coffee,' Dennis answered. 'How about you, Bryony?' he continued, turning to look at her. Bryony smiled at him, a shy and pretty smile.

'A Coke please,' she said quietly.

'A coffee and a Coke please, mate,' Dennis said, looking back at Jack.

'Coming up,' Jack said. Then, looking at Katherine, he asked, 'and you?'

'I'll come and help you,' Katherine replied, standing up smiling and winking at Jack.

After the drinks and a few laughs they decided it was time to leave, Dennis called a taxi and he, Bryony and Katherine all shared it.

Jack was lying in bed thinking about the evening that had just passed. He was very happy for his friend. Dennis and Bryony were getting on very well; they both seemed happy and relaxed in each other's company. Jack and Katherine were also getting on well, Jack was never happier than when he was with her, she made him laugh and she made him relax. He was calm with her, content. He smiled to himself in the darkness, he felt the now familiar prickling sensation starting on his body; it no longer bothered him, in fact, it bothered him so little that before anything really happened, before any hair started to grow or skin, bone and muscle started to stretch, he turned over and fell asleep.

Jack was running, the weather was bad, rain was falling in sheets, the wind was howling and it was cold and dark. The rain felt heavy on his face, his tangled wet hair seemed to be weighing him down. His running pace was slowing, the rope tied around his waist was pulling him backwards, as if it was made from elastic and had reached the point where it would stretch no more. He slowed to a walk, each step getting harder and harder, battling not only the rope, but the wind and rain as well. In front of him he could just make out a shape in the wet darkness, something hunched and animal like, the size of a large dog but more rounded, curled up. It was whimpering as though injured or lost. Jack peered through the gloom, but could not make it out. He moved a little closer, his footsteps seemed to echo in his head, he tried to make them as silent as possible, thinking it was strange he should hear them over the sound of the rain and wind. His laboured breath was also much louder than it should have been and obvious over the other noises around. The thing in front of him either heard him or caught his scent, because it stopped whimpering and lifted its head. Jack could make out two shinning eyes looking straight at him. It stood up; it was bigger than Jack, lean and cat-like. It sniffed the air, the sound reached Jack's ears. They stood looking at each other for a few seconds then the thing, whatever it was, turned and ran in the opposite direction from Jack and when he tried to follow he found he was unable to move his feet at all, it was as if they were heavy, stuck, set in concrete.

Jack woke up sweating; it was still dark, the dream had seemed so real. It had started the same as the others, but then it had changed, the weather, the feeling of the situation and he had never seen the thing he was running towards before, not even faint and blurred as it had been tonight. In the other dreams he had always been able to run, run really fast, whether running through town or country, barefoot or with shoes he had never been hindered in any of his movements. He had been free and he had been fast. The other difference was this time he had not felt as though he was running away from something, but running towards something, something he wanted to reach, something he was afraid of, but knew he had to find. And he had found it, it had been there right in front of him, only to be thwarted at the last moment by the inability to move. This time he had been the pursuer, not the pursued. Jack lay awake in the darkness, his brain refusing to relax, the dream running through his mind, it was a long while before he fell back to sleep again, but this time when he did, the sleep was dreamless.

The following day was Saturday, Jack slept late after his disturbed night. He and Katherine were meeting Dennis and Bryony at the local park that afternoon, as the fair was in town. They thought it would be fun. They met at two o'clock at the entrance and all four of them walked into the already crowded field. The weather was dry but overcast, which was a contrast to the fairground that was in full swing. The fair, with its bright lights and loud music, the rides and the stalls, all promising thrills and prizes and delivering neither. They bought candyfloss and ate it with sugary lips and sticky fingers as they walked around. Jack and Katherine went on a few rides: the big wheel, a fast roller coaster and a huge pendulum thing that went from side to side and spun around really fast, it went really high and from that highest point Jack could briefly see the whole of the fairground, which, from that height, was eerily quiet considering how busy it was. Dennis was nervous of the fast whirling and of going upside down so he and Bryony held hands and watched. After the rides, they were walking and Dennis spotted something.

'Let's go in there,' he exclaimed, pointing to a tent that had a large sign outside that read:

'Hall of Mirrors – See Yourself as Never Before
– You'll Laugh, You'll Cry.'

'Come on, it'll be a laugh,' he pleaded. They all agreed and headed for the tent. They paid their money and filed into the entrance, after the bright lights outside, their eyes took a while to become accustomed to the gloom. It was a series of small spaces; dark, but with lights over each of the mirrors which as they stood and looked at themselves, the mirrors made them look fat or thin or have a small body and huge head. They were laughing at themselves and at each other, when Jack saw a movement in the corner of the mirror he was looking in; as he looked more closely, he saw a man standing behind him, watching him. As the man realised Jack had seen him, he grinned, an evil grin that showed yellowed teeth. Jack whirled around to look behind him, but only caught the sight of a foot as it whipped out of sight. Jack felt very uneasy, who had that man been? Was he following them, or perhaps just Jack? All the way round the mirrors he kept looking for the man, in the dark corners, anywhere someone could hide, but did not see him again. They left the tent, but Jack was very wary, looking around him to see if he could see the man anywhere. He could not, not that he had got a very good look at the man's face, it had been the briefest of glances. He could not shake the feeling the man was out there though, watching him, following him and, after a couple more rides and a couple of failed attempts to win a giant teddy bear, he suggested they leave. They parted company with Dennis and Bryony at the exit, because they were heading off for tea at Bryony's parents' house.

Jack and Katherine decided to go for something to eat, they chose a small café where they enjoyed fish and chips with mushy peas and drank Coke while they chatted and laughed about the day they had just had. Jack did not mention the man in the hall of mirrors or his feeling of being watched, which still had not completely vanished, even though they had left the fair. They were so relaxed in each other's company and having such a good time, he did not want to ruin it. Jack marvelled to himself that he had ever found himself tongue-tied when he used to see Katherine. Eventually the daylight outside started to fade and lights could be seen shining brightly in the bar opposite, they could still faintly hear the sound of the fair as it continued into the evening.

Jack stood up saying, 'Come on, let me walk you home.'

Katherine stood up and together they paid the bill and walked out of the café hand in hand. They walked in comfortable silence enjoying the evening.

'Will you come over tomorrow?' Katherine asked.

'Of course, as long as you want me to,' Jack said.

Katherine smiled.

'Silly, of course I want you to.' And she hit him playfully on the shoulder, 'I still need to beat you at chess,' she added in a teasing voice.

'Never,' Jack had said, 'even if I was playing blindfolded and with both my hands tied behind my back.'

She raised her hand to give him another playful swipe, but he had already started running away from her laughing.

'I'll get you,' she called after him. 'You can run, but you can't hide.'

'You can try, but I'll always be faster than you,' he shouted back, still running.

He stopped and waited for her to catch up and then started walking again while he was still out of arms reach.

'Coward, scared of a little girl?' she teased.

'Vicious monster more like,' Jack said in a pretend frightened voice, 'those nails, or better description is claws, have always looked way too sharp to me.'

They continued in this way until they reached Katherine's front door.

'Do you want to come in?' she asked, turning to face him.

'No,' he said, 'best get home, you know how gran worries.' He rolled his eyes. Lately Pam had taken to sitting up and waiting for him to come home on the nights he went out. He knew she was feeling lonely and just wanted to spend time with him and, although he felt guilty leaving her alone, he could not stop living himself.

'Okay, see you tomorrow,' she said and standing on tip toe,

she put her arms around his neck and reached up to kiss him goodnight.

He slipped his arms around her waist and bent his head down to meet her lips. They kissed softly and then Jack broke away.

'Better go,' he said, 'see you tomorrow.'

She blew him a last kiss and turned and ran into the house. When the door was closed, Jack turned and started walking towards the bus stop, he thought to himself that he could not wait until he could start driving lessons, it would be so much easier if he had a car. As he walked he thought again about how easy it was being with Katherine; they were best friends and they had so much in common. He smiled to himself.

After a few minutes Jack came to a small alleyway, which was bordered by a high wall on one side and hedges on the other. It was a shortcut to the bus stop that he had occasionally used, though he was not very fond of the alley; it was very badly lit at night and known as something of a haven for muggers. Deciding that as it was the quickest route and that he would risk it, he started down the alley. Deep in thought, at first he did not notice the two men walking towards him until they were very close and then he only looked up and noticed them because they were talking very loudly, obviously wanting him to hear them.

'Oh look, Kev, there seems to be a little oik in our way, what should we do with 'im?' one of the men asked the other. He was tall and very skinny with oily looking hair and skin and his voice was nasal as though he had a cold.

'Dunno, Rocket, perhaps Filbert has an idea,' said the man called Kev, who was the opposite to look at to Rocket, being short and quite fat and covered in tattoos with a voice that dripped with menace, he had then looked over Jack's shoulder at something. Jack turned around quickly and saw the outline of two other men standing behind him; he could not see their faces because the only street-light was shining behind them.

One of them laughed and said with a slight Scottish accent, 'I think we all know what we do with oiks, Rocket.'

'Yeah, we squishes 'em,' the last voice, which was surprisingly high for a man, said.

Jack turned back to face the first two men again, his mind was racing, he was clearly in trouble with no way out, he could not escape forwards or backwards and the alley was not wide enough to try to run around the men. While he was still considering his limited choices, one of the men behind him grabbed both his arms and wrenched them behind his back. As he struggled against the arms that held him in a vice-like grip an iron blow hit him in the stomach and his knees gave way. Not being able to fall all the way to the ground, he dangled part way, only being held up by the man's arms. He could feel panic rising and the familiar prickling of hair growing over his body.

'What do you want?' Jack managed to rasp, though he had little breath left. 'I don't have any money,' he added.

'We're not after your money, oik,' the man called Kev said. 'We want something far more valuable than money.'

Jack did not understand what the man was saying; he did not have anything remotely valuable, unless they meant his iPhone.

'I haven't got anything...' Jack was going to add 'valuable,' but he was cut off by a second blow to the stomach and the Scottish voice saying.

'Shut up.'

'Who's got the blade?' Rocket asked, 'quick, someone might come.'

Jack's mind barely registered the word blade when he felt his left arm being pulled roughly out from his body and his sleeve rolled up, his bare arm was turned over so the inside of his wrist was exposed. He felt the cold metal briefly before the knife was pushed hard and he felt his skin give way to the sharp edge. Warm blood flowed down his arm as the knife was pulled through his skin from wrist to elbow. Jack could feel the hair still growing all down his body and the pain started in his legs as bone and flesh and muscle started contracting and stretching. In his panic a loud throaty growl escaped from his lips, this seemed to surprise the man who was holding him and his grasp slackened slightly. In that split second Jack used all the energy he could summon to try to break free, but to his surprise he felt himself being shoved away from his captor. He fell to the pavement and hit his head hard on the stony ground. As he lay there, bleeding, unsure of what was happening, he tried to think how he could get away. He thought he could hear a dog barking somewhere, though it sounded far off. He lay as still as he could, gripping the cut on his left arm with his right hand, trying to stem the flow of blood, which was heavy. He tried to clear his head, tried to use his ears and eyes to understand what was happening around him. What were the men doing, why had he been pushed to the ground? He thought he could hear shouting, though it did not sound as close as it should have, he thought he could hear people running and the barking again. At one point he thought he had seen something large and black and furry run past him and then he had heard more shouting and some screaming. Afraid the men would come back for him, Jack tried to stand up but his stomach had been hit so hard he was unable to get to his feet. He pushed himself up onto his right elbow and tried to drag himself to the wall at the side of the alley so he would at least be out of the line of fire if they returned, but as he started moving he heard something big panting behind him. Jack froze, he slowly turned his head to see the enormous black animal staring at him from a few feet away, its muzzle looking bloody and its razor sharp teeth bared. He tried to move, but none of his muscles seemed capable of movement, reminding him fleetingly of his dream when his feet seemed encased in cement although this time it was his entire body. As he watched in horror, the animal started walking slowly towards him, knowing there was no escape, Jack looked blindly around for some inspiration. None came. His head was spinning, the blood was pumping from his arm at an alarming rate and he felt dizzy and sick. The huge black animal was getting closer, it licked its bloodied lips. Jack just had time to register its strangely blue eyes, then he closed his own eyes, slumped back to the ground and everything went black.

7.

THE INTERRUPTER

'… You have to tell him, you should have told him ages ago, I told you before.'

'I know, it's hasn't been that easy, you know how hard it is.'

Jack was vaguely aware he was coming round from some sort of heavy sleep, he was definitely laying down somewhere soft and warm and he was also aware that his body was aching and sore from head to toe.

'If you don't do it today, I will.'

'Calm down, I'll do it, don't give me ultimatums. This is not your business.'

Jack could hear murmured voices, they sounded far away and muffled and almost otherworldly, like he was under water or something.

'You made it my business, you made me get involved, well, now I am and I don't like it, I don't like it at all. You're not being fair.'

The voice was female and sounded upset.

'Please calm down, I will sort this,' a male voice responded.

Jack lay listening to the voices not wanting to move in case he hurt more, actually he did not think he could hurt more, but he had been proved wrong on that score before and did not want to put it to the test.

'It's not like he has any idea, but I've seen the signs. I've seen them and I'm scared for him,' the female voice was saying.

'What signs? Why haven't you told me this before?' the male voice demanded.

'I have told you, you just don't want to hear,' the female voice again. 'I'm worried he might do something stupid because he's scared and doesn't know what's happening to him. You saw him at Christmas, you saw for yourself.'

'Listen, Jackson is a very together young man, he won't do anything stupid, he'll come to me first, I'm sure of it,' the male voice said.

Jackson? Jack thought, did he just say Jackson? Were those voices he could hear talking about him? Lying on his back he tried to move so both his ears were free of the pillow, but pain shot through his whole body. Every nerve was now alive with interest in the conversation; he strained to hear what was being said.

'He may be together, but he'll never work this one out on his own, he needs our, I mean your, help,' the female voice said.

Now Jack was listening intently, he thought the female voice sounded familiar but he could not quite put a name to it, his ears still sounded muffled and watery and the voices sounded far off.

'I've already told you, Katherine, I'll do it as soon as he wakes up.'

Katherine? Jack thought, Katherine? His Katherine? His Kat? Here? Talking about him? Who to?

'You better or I will. If the Bangers know, Jack has to.'

'It will be done today I promise, now please go home,' the male voice said.

The conversation appeared to have ended, Jack was trying to remember what had been said; something about how he should have been told something and how he might do something stupid and some bangers, whatever that meant. How he wished his mind had been clearer and that he had listened harder, none of this made any sense to him.

Looking around the room, Jack realised he was in the hospital, the same hospital, by the look of it, that he'd had his operation in, could even be the same room, hard to tell as they all looked the same. Taking a deep breath and readying himself for the onslaught of pain, he moved slightly onto his right side and reached for the call button, wondering for umpteenth time why they could not put it nearer the centre of the bed. Pain rushed through every part of him, but nowhere as badly as his left arm, which seemed to sear with agony. It felt as though it was being ripped off half way down. He lay back onto his back quickly, holding his breath and gritting his teeth and waiting for the pain to subside. He noticed, through water-filled eyes, that his left arm was thickly bandaged from his wrist to his elbow. As he was contemplating what could be under the bandage, a nurse came in the door.

'Hi,' she said, 'feeling rough?'

'Yes,' Jack croaked. 'Terrible.'

'Thought so,' she said kindly, 'I'll give you some painkillers.'

As she reached for his right hand, Jack realised he was on a drip.

'What happened to me?' he asked.

'You were attacked,' she said quietly, 'try not to think about it.'

'No... but... what? Attacked?' Jack could feel panic rising in his stomach. Attacked? No, surely that had been a dream? Really? Attacked?

'Please, try not to worry,' the nurse said, now sounding worried herself.

'No, I... I... I need to know,' Jack stuttered.

'Not now,' the nurse said. 'Go back to sleep and the doctor will be up to see you later.'

Jack tried to say, 'No, I want to see the doctor now,' except nothing came out but a soft murmur; he felt the painkillers numbing his body and he fell into an irresistible sleep.

Jack awoke abruptly; he had been dreaming, running again, although, as ever, it was not quite the same as before. Try as he might, Jack could not remember the details of the dream, which was unusual and frustrating. Usually, he remembered the dreams with startling clarity, but today it eluded him. He lay staring at the ceiling, hoping the doctor would be around soon and wondering if he was going to explain the conversation Jack had overheard earlier. The word 'bangers' kept going round his head, what could that possibly mean? Bangers? Jack lay there for what seemed like ages until eventually the door opened and Dr Noah walked in.

'Jackson,' Dr Noah said. 'If you are feeling up to it, I need to talk to you. There are some things I need to explain to you, about, well, you and why you were attacked.'

Jack pushed himself carefully into a sitting position, pain now playing second fiddle to curiosity, listening intently, his eyes fixed on the doctor's eyes.

'Before I start,' the doctor continued, 'please understand this isn't easy to explain, it's going to sound strange and impossible, but I beg you to hear me out. I want you know I have your best interests at heart. If I should have come to you before now and explained, um, things, then I'm sorry. I thought you would come to me, I thought, well, maybe I hoped, we had a, well, a friendship of sorts. I don't know.'

The doctor seemed to almost be talking to himself. He looked confused, no, more than that, he looked worried, almost scared, as though he did not want to be talking but had no choice.

He looked at Jack, his face looked older somehow, more lined, his expression pained. After a few seconds he said, 'Firstly I need to ask you if anything out of the ordinary has happened to you lately?'

'You mean other than being attacked?' Jack asked.

'Yes, I mean has anything unusual or strange happened to you? Things that you cannot explain?'

Jack looked at the doctor, he was not sure what to say, now was the perfect time to unburden himself, tell Dr Noah everything, but then again, he just was not sure. What if he told Dr Noah everything and that was not what the doctor had meant.

'I don't know what you mean,' Jack said.

Dr Noah looked at him for a few seconds.

'Okay, well, I'll start. I'll try to explain but this won't be easy,' the doctor said.

'Okay,' Jack agreed, still holding the doctor's eyes eagerly. Was he about to get all the answers he had been looking for? The answers for the dreams, the changes, the newfound energy, the extra fast healing?

'Jackson, I've been following your life since you were born, watching you grow and struggle with your ill health,' Dr Noah started.

'Since I was born?' Jack whispered.

'Yes, since you were a baby.' The doctor continued, 'I've been keeping an eye on you because I knew you were... special... or different,' he said. 'The thing is, and Jackson, again, I beg you listen. The thing is, you are special and different. You are not an ordinary boy, I mean, man,' he corrected. 'You may well be aware of that by now, if you have been experiencing the, well, unusual things I think you have, anyway, to put it bluntly you are what we call a morpher.'

There were a few seconds of clanging silence where Jack stared at the doctor and the doctor stared at the wall.

'A whater?' asked Jack, not understanding the word at all. 'What's a morpher?'

'A morpher,' the doctor said, still not meeting Jack's eyes, 'is someone who can change their physical appearance at will, that is to say they can change into another form or being if they so choose.' Finally he looked at Jack, 'With me so far?' he asked.

'I think so,' said Jack cautiously, his heart thumping wildly, 'although I've never heard of a morpher. Why haven't I heard of morphers?'

'Well, they're not very common; less than one per cent of the population are morphers and we don't brag about it, we keep it quiet,' Dr Noah said.

'We?' asked Jack. 'Er, you mean... er, are you saying... um, that... are you a morpher?' Jack asked incredulously.

'Well, yes I am,' Dr Noah answered simply.

Jack stared at him with his mouth open, Dr Noah did not seem the type to play tricks or tell jokes, he looked deadly serious, but this was ridiculous – Dr Noah, a strange person who can change their appearance at will?

'I'm not sure what you mean by 'change their appearance at will'.' Jack said. 'Change their appearance to what?'

'Well, that depends on the individual,' the doctor explained. 'Everyone is different, Jackson. Some find they can morph into, well, animals; you know, cats, dogs, horses, that sort of thing. Some can only morph into one specific animal, they have no choice about the animal and others can choose from several different animals or species of animals.'

'Animals?' Jack interrupted thoughtfully. He was thinking of the changes he had experienced, his body parts changing shape, now he thought about it, all the changes he had seen had looked animal-ish, particularly the fur and the stumpy tail thing. He felt a bit sick and faint; this was so weird.

'Not just animals; like I said, everyone is different.' The doctor continued, 'Some don't morph into animals at all, some can morph to look like other people, though they are rare, even amongst morphers.' He looked at Jack who was looking shocked and pale.

'Are you okay Jackson?' he asked.

'Yes,' said Jack, he did not want the doctor to stop. 'How did you know I was a morpher when I was born?' he asked.

'There are signs,' the doctor explained.

'So,' said Jack, his mind was spinning. 'Why haven't I ever changed into anything?'

'I'm sure you have experienced some physical changes, even if they are only small ones?' Dr Noah asked.

'How do you know?' Jack asked.

'I've seen the signs, Christmas at your house for one.'

'Oh,' said Jack.

'Most morphers don't change completely into, well whatever it is they turn into, until they reach their teens, everyone is different so some start earlier and some later. The problem with you was your heart wasn't strong enough to cope with the morphing process, that's why we needed the operation; I was concerned that if you morphed with your old heart you wouldn't be strong enough to morph back, you could have been stuck as, whatever you had changed into, or worse you could have died,' Dr Noah explained.

Jack had a sudden thought, 'What about my new heart?' he asked.

'It came from a morpher, yes,' the doctor confirmed.

'Really, the man who was hit by the lorry, he was a morpher? How do you know?' Jack asked.

'I knew him,' Dr Noah said simply.

'I'm sorry,' said Jack feeling guilty.

'I'm sorry too.' Dr Noah replied. 'But he would have been glad his heart went to you, glad that it went to a good home.'

'Why didn't you tell me all this before?' Jack asked.

'I wasn't sure if everything would still be in working order after the operation; I've never transplanted a morphers heart into a morpher before, for all I knew, it could have completely taken away all your ability, I wanted to make sure you could still morph before I filled you in. It would have been cruel to tell you all this and then find you couldn't do it,' Dr Noah said, 'I kept a close eye on you. I was sure if anything strange happened to you, you would tell me and then I could tell you the truth, but you wouldn't tell me anything.' He looked at Jack with mock sternness.

'Sorry,' said Jack, 'I didn't know what to think. I was scared, but it felt very personal; I didn't want to tell anyone.'

'Understandable,' Dr Noah said kindly.

'So what will I change into?' Jack asked, suddenly feeling excited.

'I don't know,' the doctor said, 'it's a case of wait and find out, I'm afraid.'

'What do you change into?' Jack asked, not sure if the doctor would answer.

'Ah, I'm a rare morpher. Before I tell you, I will tell you this: I don't morph very often, in fact, it's been over twenty years.'

'Why so long?' asked Jack.

'Well, as I'm sure you have already experienced, morphing can be very painful, the larger or smaller the shape you take the more painful it is, that's because you have to either grow or shrink your bones, muscles and skin. It can be agony.' Dr Noah explained. 'I am a monoskin which means I can only morph to one animal and it's a very large one; when I change, I become an elephant.'

Jack had a weird urge to laugh and had to clamp his lips together to stop himself, even though it was not really funny.

'Wow,' he said.

'Exactly,' the doctor said, 'but an animal that size is torturous to become; it's so painful that, unless there is very good reason, I don't do it.'

They sat in silence for a while, Jack was trying to imagine Dr Noah as an elephant and felt the urge to laugh again; he wished it had been a smaller animal so he could demonstrate it to Jack, but evidently this was not an option.

Dr Noah cleared this throat. Jack looked up.

'Any questions?' he asked.

Yes, a million.

'No,' said Jack.

If Dr Noah was surprised, he did not show it.

'Even though morphers can change into another shape – say, a cat – the whole body changes with the exception of the eyes. The eyes, Jackson, they never change, they can really give you away because they remain human. Most morphers who can choose what they change into will choose something like a dog. There are two reasons for this: firstly, it is a medium-sized animal, so it's less painful than, say, an elephant,' Dr Noah smiled, 'or a mouse. But also, because dog's eyes are quite similar to human eyes, in that they have round pupils, so they look less out of place. With me so far?' Dr Noah asked.

'Yes, I think so,' Jack said thoughtfully, he was remembering trying to change the colour of his eyes and getting frustrated when he could not.

'Do emotions have anything to do with morphing?' Jack asked, a little embarrassed.

'They can do, particularly when you're young and not used to it. A lot of teenagers find they can't always control the changes that occur when they are angry or sad, but as you get more used to morphing, you will get better at controlling it,' the doctor advised. 'Okay, so, now you know what you are, it will take a lot of practise when you find out what you can morph into but practice makes perfect. One thing I would advise, if you are lucky enough to be a polyskin, which means you are able to change into several different things, be careful to choose real things, like real animals. If you try to morph into either something made-up, or a cross between two animals, it can be catastrophic,' Dr Noah said.

'Why?' asked Jack.

'Well, with a real animal, your brain knows exactly what is

expected: fur, four legs, pointy ears, you get the picture. With something made-up or a hybrid, your brain has to interpret what you want and it needs to do it exactly. If anything goes even slightly wrong, your brain and the interrupter will both start working extra hard to put it right and they can start working against each other. I'm not saying it can't be done, I'm just saying you have to be very careful and it's certainly not recommended until you are very competent at morphing.' The doctor looked at Jack and said, 'I must say, you are taking this very calmly; you're very accepting of such a strange truth.'

'I guess I'm just glad to know I'm not going mad,' Jack admitted. 'I was worried that I was either losing my mind or going through some hideous transformation because I was a freak. It feels good to know I'm not the only one.' There was silence for a while then Jack added, 'What's an interrupter?'

'Ah, now, if you look at your left arm.' Dr Noah continued.

Jack looked at the bandage.

'You were attacked last night because someone tried to steal the disc that is under the skin on your wrist,' Dr Noah said.

Jack looked at the doctor in shock.

'Someone wanted to steal that disc-thing?' he asked.

'That disc-thing, or interrupter as it's correctly called, is a very valuable object. I'm sorry, Jackson, I wasn't very honest with you when you asked me before what it did. It doesn't monitor your pulse, it's a lot more important than that.' Dr Noah explained, 'When someone morphs into a new shape, particularly an animal, every part of their body becomes that animal, with, as I mentioned before, the exception of the eyes. The eyes are the only exception, though, the only one. This causes a very major problem; the human brain is very advanced and capable of very complex thoughts. Animals' brains are much simpler; they rely a lot on instinct and, although they have memories and some can even be problem-solving, they cannot cope with the scope that the human brain is used to. If someone morphs into an animal, their mind starts to become like that of the animal they look like; the longer they stay as that animal, the more the mind becomes simpler, to the point where if the morpher remains as the animal for too long, they will start to forget being human and eventually will be unable to cope with the thoughts that would allow them to morph back to their human form. Still with me?'

'I think so,' said Jack, his head spinning.

'Well, the interrupter is designed to maintain human thought while morphed; it has the ability to keep your human mind in whatever body you are in so, no matter how long you remain as an animal, you will always think like a human, like yourself, and always have the ability to morph back, understand?' Dr Noah asked.

'Yes,' said Jack, 'the disc-thing lets morphers stay as animals longer than without it and still become human again.'

'Correct,' said the doctor. 'Any questions.'

'Yes,' Jack said looking at his right wrist, that too had a bandage on it, 'what happened to this arm?'

Dr Noah looked even more serious.

'It's likely that someone may try to steal your interrupter again, if they succeed, it could be very dangerous for you. I've fitted a sort of mini interrupter on your other wrist as a sort of back-up; it should allow you to morph normally if you need to, it will give you some time before you can get to me to have a new one fitted on your left wrist, it's very small, no one should be able to spot it, it should be safe.'

'Oh, thanks,' Jack said, almost automatically. This was too much to take in.

'Kat,' Jack said, mainly to himself.

'I'm sorry?' asked Dr Noah, 'Cat?'

'I mean Katherine, she has a disc, an interrupter thing.' He looked at Dr Noah, 'Is Katherine a morpher too?'

Dr Noah was silent for a moment.

'I'm sure Katherine would rather tell you this herself, but yes, she is.'

Jack was stunned, all this time he had known her and he'd had no idea she had this enormous secret, just like he had no idea he also had the same enormous secret.

'Does Kat, I mean Katherine, does she know about me?' Jack asked.

'Yes, she's been helping me keep an eye on you.' Dr Noah said.

I bet she has, Jack thought, feeling his temper start to rise.

'Brilliant,' he said sarcastically.

'Don't feel bad and don't think badly of Katherine. Talk to her, she'll explain,' the doctor said. 'Anymore questions?'

'Yes,' said Jack, looking up. 'Why would someone want to steal my disc, what about their own?'

'Ah, well, not everyone has an interrupter. They are given to most morphers because they use their ability for some good purpose or just for fun, but there are those who like to turn their talents to wrong-doing and would be able to break far more laws for their own personal gain without the chance of detection, if they could remain as animals indefinitely.'

'You say they *tried* to steal it? Does that mean they didn't actually take it?' asked Jack.

'No, they must have been disturbed, they wouldn't normally stop mid-attack.' Doctor Noah said thoughtfully.

'The dog,' Jack said quietly, almost to himself.

'What dog?' asked the doctor.

'A big, black dog,' Jack explained, 'I sort of remember being on the ground and then I think I saw this big dog, it came running up the alley, growling. Then it came towards me, but I can't remember anything after that. It must have been the dog...' he trailed off.

There was silence for a while, then Jack asked.

'Who decides who gets a disc and who doesn't?'

'I do,' said Dr Noah, 'I invented the interrupter and I fit them. Unfortunately the people who try to steal them have become quite good at fitting them themselves now, which is a pity. The problem they have is that each interrupter is designed specifically for the individual I fit it to, therefore they are not always compatible with the new morpher.'

'What happens if they aren't compatible?' asked Jack.

'They don't work, they have no effect at all in prolonging the human mind; this would obviously not show until it was too late, but there are physical signs as well. It's similar to when a body rejects a donor organ: infection, sickness, you know,' replied the doctor.

'Who are these people?' asked Jack.

'They are a gang of men,' Dr Noah said. 'They are villains, mainly thieves and con-men, they are violent and they don't care about hurting anyone. You can see the appeal; small animals can get into tiny places, which would make breaking into a house or a bank easier. Then when the robbery is done, stay as the animal until the heat dies down and, best of all, no finger prints.'

'Who are these men?' Jack asked, horrified.

'They call themselves the Bangers,' the doctor replied.

Jack spent two days in hospital. Pam had been desperate for news when Jack had not come home on the night of the attack. Dr Noah had phoned her as soon as Jack had been admitted and she had come straight to the hospital, even though it was three in the morning. She had wanted to stay at the hospital until Jack was released, but Jack had insisted that she get proper rest at home, saying he would need her to be strong to look after him when they let him go. Pam had not bought the story, but had done as he wished, though would not give up visiting him twice a day.

It had been quite awkward the first time Katherine had visited Jack the evening after Dr Noah had told him the truth about himself. As she had walked through the door and caught his eye, he had given her a look that said, *you are a traitor* and she had burst into tears.

'I'm so sorry, Jack. I wanted to tell you, I really did. I begged Uncle Leo to let me tell you,' Katherine sobbed.

'So you were just keeping an eye on me for your uncle?' Jack accused. 'Is that why you were nice to me, because your Uncle Leo asked you to be?'

'No,' she looked horrified. 'Yes he asked me to watch out for you, yes he asked me to report back if I thought anything was happening to you, but he never asked me to get to know you, only watch you from a distance. I liked you, Jack, from the moment I first saw you, I liked you. I wanted to get to know you, my choice, Jack, mine.' She was still crying and looked like she may never stop.

'Really?' Jack asked sarcastically.

'Yes, really,' she replied. 'What sort of girl do you think I am?'

'A dishonest one,' Jack had said meanly. 'One that could have told me the truth, one who spent time with me knowing a huge secret about both of us and never letting me get to know her at all,' he finished.

She looked at him with her sad eyes; she had stopped crying.

'Please understand, I couldn't tell you. You have no idea how much I wanted to. Of course I wanted to tell you about me. I can't tell anyone.' She started crying again.

They were both silent apart from the sobbing sounds. Jack was watching her, her head was bowed into her lap, he wanted to believe her, but he really wished she could have confided in him, just a few bits, if not everything.

'So,' he said finally, 'what do you become when you, you know, morph-thingy?'

She looked up.

'Didn't Uncle Leo tell you?' she whispered.

'No, he said you would want to tell me yourself…' he trailed off. This was surreal.

She smiled.

'Look into my eyes, Jack, don't you know these eyes?' she asked.

He stared into her eyes, her startling bluish-green eyes. *The eyes never change*, the voice in his head reminded him. Where had he seen those eyes before? He moved closer to get a better look.

'Unusual colour,' he murmured.

'Come on, Jack, you know these eyes,' she encouraged.

'I don't know, maybe,' Jack said, feeling a bit frustrated.

She smiled again through her watery eyes.

'I'm Poppy,' she admitted.

'Poppy?' Jack repeated. 'You're Poppy?'

So that explained why Poppy had never come round to his house when Katherine had been there. He had been desperate for them to meet and had called to Poppy many times trying to encourage her in when Katherine had been there.

'You must have thought me an idiot when I called for Poppy to come and meet you,' he said slightly sulkily.

'No, I thought it was so sweet that you wanted us to meet,' she assured him.

'But I've known Poppy for ages, years, much longer than I've known you, how come?' Jack asked.

'As you know, Uncle Leo asked me to keep an eye on you. It was much easier as a cat than as a human, you must be able to see that?' She replied.

'Hmm,' Jack said. 'But you moved here from somewhere abroad, how could you be Poppy?'

'That wasn't exactly the truth, Jack,' Katherine said in small voice.

'Another lie to add to all the others,' Jack said bitterly. 'Wish you'd told me sooner though.'

'I know,' she said quietly, 'I'm sorry, I wish I had too.'

'But, hang on, like I said, I've known Poppy for years, how can you be her? Dr Noah, your Uncle Leo, said the whole morphing thing usually starts when people reach their teens, you would have had to have been much younger than that?'

'Yes, well, I started morphing before I learned to walk and talk, which is rare, though not unheard of, that's one of the reasons Uncle Leo asked for my help; we were the same age, you see, he thought I would understand you.'

They sat in silence for a while, not looking at each other, both feeling a bit awkward and shy. Eventually Jack looked at Katherine and said, 'Can you only change into Poppy?' Jack asked, 'Dr Noah told me that he can only change into an elephant, can you only change into a cat?'

'Yes,' said Katherine, 'I'm a monoskin, like Uncle Leo, though I'm luckier because I'm a cat,' she added.

'Do you think I'll be a monoskin?' Jack asked.

'I don't know,' Katherine replied.

'What do you think I'll, you know, change into?' he sounded a bit concerned.

'I don't know, Jack,' Katherine replied, 'everyone is different. When you experienced some of the early changes, what did it look like?'

'Dunno,' said Jack thoughtfully, 'definitely furry, and I think I had some sort of tail,' he added with a slight shudder.

Katherine smiled.

'Finding the tail painful?' she asked.

'Agony,' Jack replied, 'agony to grow and agony to touch.'

'It gets easier,' Katherine assured him. 'It's like anything, the more you do it, the easier it becomes.'

'Yeah, well, I'm not sure I want to do that too often,' Jack grumbled.

She smiled, her pretty face still streaked with tears.

'We'll see,' she said.

8.

A Hard Lesson

'So, what do you think?' Jack asked, standing in front of Katherine with both his arms spread wide.

'I think you're not concentrating,' she replied, half amused, half exasperated. 'One thing's for sure though, you're definitely a polyskin.'

'How can you tell?' Jack asked eagerly.

'Well, unless I'm very much mistaken, you have one furry leg and one that looks a lot like feathers and I don't know about you, but I've never seen an animal like that before.'

Jack looked down at his legs and sure enough, one was furry and one was feathery. Now he thought about it, the feathery one had been a lot more painful to change than the furry one, he supposed that was due to feathers being a lot thicker than hairs to grow. He looked back at Katherine.

'Why does that mean I'm a polyskin?' he asked.

'Because if you can grow fur and feathers you must be able to turn into mammals and birds,' she said simply.

'Oh yeah,' Jack said. *Excellent*, he thought.

They had been in his bedroom practising morphing for the last two hours. Katherine had been demonstrating how she was able to very easily, and very quickly, morph into Poppy and back again. It seemed to take her hardly any time at all and from the lack of screaming, it did not seem very painful either.

'I've had a lot of practise,' she said, almost apologetically, 'I've been doing this since I was a baby. It's as natural to me as walking. Don't beat yourself up, you'll get the hang of it.'

But he was not getting the hang of it, Katherine had been helping him ever since he had returned home from the hospital, but so far he was not any further morphing into a real animal than he had been before the attack. He looked at himself in the mirror; his body was definitely that of a large dog. His arms were both furry and were sort of a cross between dog and human, though one definitely had a paw. His legs, as Katherine had pointed out, were a mismatch of dog and bird. His face, still human, was furry and his teeth were pointy. There was no tail; he refused to even try to grow one, the pain was so intense.

'You know you never will become a complete dog until you embrace the tail,' Katherine said, 'the more you avoid it, the harder it will become.'

He knew she was right; every time he tried to concentrate on changing into a dog (they had chosen a dog to start with because that was what he most resembled when bits of him morphed), he would think of a dog very clearly in his mind, picturing every part of its body, he would feel all the changes starting to happen, but as soon as he felt the sharp pain start in the base of his spine, he would quickly try to think of an animal that did not have a tail. Today he had thought of an eagle, though quite why, he did not know because, obviously, birds do have tails, and this would cause the morphing process to halt part way through. Ever aware of Dr Noah's warning not to try to morph into a hybrid until he was more proficient at the whole process, he would immediately try to stop any more changes taking place before he caused himself any damage and so always ended up a part-dog. Today was, however, the first time he had grown feathers and he found that very exciting; if he could grow feathers, then maybe he could morph into a bird of some sort and, if he could become a bird, well, then surely it stood to reason that he might be able to *fly*. Concentrating with all his mind, he changed back into himself and he sat down on the bed next to Katherine.

'Maybe we shouldn't have chosen a dog,' he suggested, 'maybe I need to start with something that doesn't have a tail?'

'Like what?' Katherine asked. 'Okay, some cats don't have tails and some dogs, but usually they have been cut off and therefore they still have stumps,' she pointed out.

They went through every animal they could think of, but could not come up with anything that did not have some sort of tail, even if it was a very small and skinny one.

'I'm never going to be able to do this,' Jack sighed.

The next day, when Jack was at work, a black Labrador was brought in who had been hit by a car and left at the side of the road; a passing motorist had found him and brought him to the shelter. No one knew who he belonged to, but he was in bad way and needed immediate treatment. Mr Fielding was called and he rushed home to see what the injured dog needed. After examining the poor animal, he told Nora and Jack that he would have to operate.

'Must have been hit with quite some force,' he told them, 'his back legs are both broken and he has four broken ribs and multiple cuts. Poor thing must have been in agony, I've sedated him, I must start work straight away.'

And with that he disappeared into his surgery. Jack and Nora went back to work, though neither could concentrate; Jack could not believe anyone could hit an animal with a car and just leave it. They both went about their duties waiting for news of the poor dog, in the absence of knowing the dog's real name they had decided to call him Charlie, because Nora said he looked like a Charlie. Two hours later Mr Fielding appeared to tell them that Charlie was doing well, his broken bones had been set and his cuts had been stitched; unfortunately, the bones in one of his back legs had literally been crushed and had therefore been too badly damaged and Mr Fielding had had no choice but to amputate.

'He'll be fine though,' Mr Fielding assured them, 'you'll be amazed how animals compensate for losing limbs and such. They adapt much better than people, we rely too much on crutches, prosthetics and wheelchairs. Animals, well, they just get on with it, you'll see.'

Jack had not been so sure at the time, but was amazed that just a few weeks later Charlie was walking around on three legs like he had been doing it all his life. Jack and Charlie had become good friends. When Charlie had woken up after the operation, he had been disorientated and frightened and had growled quite viciously when Mr Fielding or Nora had tried to get anywhere near him. Nora had immediately called Jack.

'Jack, can you please go and make a very gentle fuss of Charlie, he's scared and needs a bit of love and reassurance,' she said, then she looked at her Dad. 'Watch this,' she told him.

Jack went over to Charlie who watched him warily for a few seconds, but made no sound and then seemed to just wait for his approach. Jack gently stroked his head, trying to avoid anywhere that looked like it might hurt, and murmured soft words of encouragement.

'Hey boy, how you doing? You okay, boy?' he said, very softly and slowly and the dog just lay there, appearing to enjoy it.

'Amazing,' said Mr Fielding, 'you certainly have a gift with animals, Jack, ever thought of being a vet?'

Jack looked over to Mr Fielding and Nora.

'Oh, I'd love to be a vet,' he said, 'wasn't good enough at school though, I'm afraid'

'Pity,' said Mr Fielding. 'Well I must get back to work, I'll leave our patient in your capable hands.'

So a few weeks on they still did not know Charlie's real name or who he belonged to. Mr Fielding said he must have an owner because he was well looked after and certainly would not have been so healthy if he had been a stray. Jack really wanted take Charlie home with him but he knew his grandma would never allow a dog in the house, that thought had made him laugh to himself – if only she knew!

If Jack had thought the actual morphing was the difficult bit, he had been very much mistaken. Having finally mastered the full change into a dog, albeit a dog without a tail, because Jack had decided this was definitely enough pain and that the tail was unnecessary anyway, he was not however prepared for the even harder task that was in front of him.

'Well if Charlie can manage with only three legs,' he had said to Katherine, 'then surely I can at least try it without a tail.'

Which he had, picturing very clearly a dog, like Charlie, but with four legs and no tail and found it to be a lot easier. It allowed him to keep going. When the pain in the base of his spine started, he simply concentrated even harder on the dog being tailless and that particular pain subsided. Of course there was still all the other pains, but he was getting more used to those and was learning to put up with them. That said, the full transformation had taken him nearly twenty-three minutes to complete compared to Katherine, who could manage the full change in less than one minute.

'You'll get quicker,' she assured him, 'Practice makes perfect.'

Once Jack was completely a dog though, he'd had a huge shock, well, two huge shocks actually. Firstly, he was no longer able to talk; animal voice boxes are not equipped for human speech, something he had not even thought about. Even though he had spent time with Katherine as Poppy, he only just realised she had never spoken as a cat, only meowed and purred! The second shock came when Jack tried to walk and it was a far worse shock than the first one. As he tried to put one foot in front of the other, he was suddenly aware that he had twice as many legs and feet than he was used to and they sort of got all tangled up and he stumbled and nearly fell. He had looked up at Katherine questioningly and she had laughed.

'Jack, you didn't think you would just become a dog and run off and do doggy things just like that, did you? You didn't think walking and running as an animal was going to just happen, did you, without any help or practice?'

But he had, he had assumed that once he had the animal shape and body, he would be like that animal. He sat, rather awkwardly, not really sure where all the legs were supposed to go. He looked up at her and something of what he was feeling must have shown in his doggy face because she stopped laughing and said kindly.

'Oh, Jack. If you bought a pair of roller-skates, would you expect to put them on and just be able to skate? No, you would expect to have to learn how to move with wheels on your feet and then you would expect that the more practice you had, the less wobbly you would become until you got better and better and eventually you'd be able to skate well. Well it's the same with this; as a human you have only two legs and you're used to walking like that. As a dog, you have four legs and you have to learn the order they go in when you walk, it will take a while until it feels natural.'

This was not what Jack wanted to hear, he had assumed, obviously naively, that once he had taken the form of an animal, any animal, the movements would be easy, instinctual even. On a positive note his sense of smell was definitely stronger, even more so than normal; having experienced a heightened sense of smell following his heart operation, he could now distinguish even more aromas. Although in his bedroom, he could very clearly smell the grass on the lawn outside, an array of foodie smells coming from the kitchen downstairs, which were making him feel hungry, and some chemical smells coming from the bathroom. The other positive note was that his hearing was also intensified; he could hear sounds that seemed to come from miles away, though they were hard to distinguish. He could hear cars going past on the road – not something he could usually hear from his room because the main road was at least half a mile from his house and on the other side to his bedroom. All this information at once was too much for Jack; he morphed back to human, although this process was easier than morphing to an animal, it was still quite painful and took almost fifteen minutes. Once human again, Jack sat on the bed feeling exhausted and fed up. Katherine sat beside him.

'Don't feel too down, Jack,' she said.

'Why not?' Jack asked, slightly bitterly. 'It's okay for you, this is all easy for you.'

'I'm sorry,' Katherine said sadly staring at the floor. 'It's only easy for me because I've been doing this for years. I'm also lucky, I was so young I don't really remember the pain and the learning, like most people don't remember the pain of growing teeth or learning to walk or talk. It will come, Jack, you just need to practice and be patient. It will come and it will be worth it.'

She looked at Jack. 'Please don't hate me,' she added.

Jack looked into Katherine's eyes, her beautiful, unusual blue-green eyes.

'I don't hate you,' he said, and, without thinking, he added, 'I could never hate you, I love you.'

Katherine drew in a sharp breath. 'You do?' she breathed.

Jack, realising he had said it out loud, could feel his heart start to race. He looked at the floor.

'Yes,' he said in a small voice. He looked at her questioningly.

Katherine smiled, a small smile to start with, but it grew bigger and wider.

'I love you,' she whispered. 'I love you so much, I always have, ever since I first saw you.'

She laughed, Jack smiled and then they were in each other's arms, kissing and laughing.

Practice makes perfect kept running through Jack's mind three weeks later. He had to admit it did seem to be getting easier every time he tried to morph. He had kept to the tailless dog, not wanting to try any other animal and risk ruining his concentration, and had got the entire process from first tingles of fur to complete transformation down to twelve minutes, twelve minutes of still quite intense pain, but at least it was getting quicker. Walking on four legs was still posing a bit of a problem; Jack had got over the initial issue of not being able to move and was at least walking, but his walk was slow and awkward and must have looked to onlookers as though he was drunk. He swayed and stumbled and moved with the intense concentration of a person under the influence of alcohol, but trying desperately not to show it. He knew Katherine was desperate for him to be confident enough to venture outside with her as Poppy and him as a dog.

'We must think of a name for you as a dog,' she had said one day when he was stumbling around his bedroom on four furry legs.

'If I'm Poppy, who can you be?' she had asked him thoughtfully.

Fine time to ask me a question, he had thought, *when I'm concentrating on trying to learn how to walk and, even if I wasn't, I can't speak as a dog anyway.* But this did get him thinking, his dog-self did need an identity, and a name would make that easier. He quickly dismissed all the common names most people give their pets and decided he needed something more fitting to him. *What though?* He thought, as he continued to walk round his room.

At that moment, Katherine squealed, 'Jack, you're doing it, you're doing it.'

He stopped walking and looked at her questioningly.

'You're walking, well, you were. I mean, properly walking, not falling or stumbling, but actually walking. You did it, Jack!'

So he had. All the time he had been concentrating on walking, he had been very wobbly, but as soon as his mind had wandered onto other things – like trying to think of a suitable name – he had walked perfectly. *Over concentration did not help,* he thought, *must remember that.* He morphed back to human; it took him a mere eight minutes. He hugged Katherine.

'Well done,' she said, her eyes shining. 'You see, practice, that's all you needed, we'll be able to go outside together soon. You'll love it, Jack, out there.'

Jack still thought a cat and a tailless dog might look a little odd walking down the street together, but he had to admit, the thought of getting out into the fresh air and learning to stretch his legs was really appealing.

It felt weird but wonderful; the wind was blowing and Jack's fur was rippling, the ground was hard and stony, his bare paws could feel every little stone or crack though it did not hurt like it sometimes did with bare human feet. The air was fresh and sweet, the wind brought with it interesting smells, smells Jack had never experienced before, he could not recognise most of them. Poppy trotted beside him, looking up at him every few seconds. He was walking slowly, not just because he was nervous, but also because he wanted to take everything in, Katherine had been right, she had said he would love it outside and he did. It was not like being outside as a human. For one thing, he was seeing everything from a much lower level; walking on four legs his head was only about three feet from the ground, he was used to seeing things at twice that height. For another thing, he was barefoot and naked; he had certainly never walked down the street without clothes on before, it felt weird and a bit embarrassing, but a tailless dog wearing jeans and a t-shirt would certainly draw attention!

It was Jack's first venture outside as Prince, the tailless dog.

They had finally decided on Prince as Jack's doggy name only the night before. Using Jack's surname King as inspiration, they had both been delighted to come up with a name that meant something, had a doggy feel to it and had started with the letter P – the same as Poppy. Jack had felt a lot more comfortable once his tailless dog had an identity; he felt like it was more real, like Prince actually existed, was a being in his own right, the way Jack had always thought of Poppy.

Poppy and Prince, Prince and Poppy, it had a good feel to it, they sounded right together. With the name agreed on, Katherine was quick to suggest that it was time for Prince to go outside.

'Come on, Jack,' she had pleaded. 'You have to go outside sometime, you will really enjoy it, it's so much better than when you're human, so much, oh I don't know, freer.'

Jack had been a bit reluctant, he was not sure he was ready. Okay, so he could morph in less than ten minutes, not as quick as he would like, but certainly getting quicker all the time. And he could walk now; in fact, he could walk quite quickly without getting his legs tangled up or even wobbling drunkenly. But that had all been done in the safety of his bedroom, where no one could see him, except Katherine, of course. Outside was a whole new experience, bringing with it excitement, but also danger. After a lot of persuasion by Katherine, he had finally agreed.

'Okay, okay,' he had finally said, holding both hands up in mock surrender. 'I'll go, I'll go. But only as far as the end of the road and back again,' he added. 'I just want to try it first, get my bearings.'

'Of course, whatever you say,' Katherine had replied, a big smile on her pretty face.

Now he was outside however, although slightly nervous, he was more relaxed than he had imagined he would be, it felt nice – it felt natural. They got to the end of the road, he looked down at Poppy, who was looking up at him, and he could have sworn she was smiling smugly, as if she knew what he was thinking. She looked behind herself in the direction they had just walked, then she looked forward in the direction they were walking, then she looked at Prince. It could not have been clearer what she was trying to say: *Do you want to go home or do you want to go on?* Jack laughed, although what came out was a sort of half bark. He looked forwards and sniffed. Poppy took this as a sign he wanted to go further and she started forward, Jack waited a couple of seconds and then followed. They walked on for a few minutes and then Poppy took a right turn down a small lane. Jack knew what was at the end of that lane, a field. He felt excited and then laughed at himself, thinking he was like a real dog getting excited at going for walkies!

The grass felt wonderful under paw, it was soft and cool and slightly damp, much nicer than the pavement had been. Prince walked tentatively for a few steps, getting the feel of this new, strange land before he started moving a little bit quicker. Poppy watched from the side of the field as Prince gained speed; a bit faster, a bit faster still, a very fast walk, which made his furry bottom wiggle, a bit faster until, eventually, he broke into a slow run. Ever since his operation Jack had loved running, had loved the feeling of moving fast on his feet, the wind in his hair, but it had never felt as good as this – he felt like he could run forever.

He suddenly realised Poppy was at his side, she had run across the grass to join him and was keeping pace with him as he ran across the soft grass. He sped up trying to out-run her. He looked to his side to see if she was still there and as he did so, he tripped over a tree root that was sticking up out of the earth. His furry legs got tangled up and he went flying, all four feet off the ground.

'Ow,' Jack said.

'Hold still,' Katherine replied.

'But it hurts,' Jack complained.

'Stop being such a baby,' Katherine laughed.

They were in Jack's kitchen and Katherine was dabbing iodine on Jack's bloody legs and arms.

After Prince's very spectacular flying fall, they had limped home with Prince whimpering on every step. He had landed badly, grazing all his limbs against a tree trunk, but, with no clothes to hand, he had been forced to keep Prince's form until they had got home, where both Jack and Katherine had been able to morph back to human. The morphing had been even more painful than ever with his bleeding wounds and now Katherine was making them all hurt even more. Jack was not in a good mood.

Katherine looked at him, smiling.

'Have you ever heard the expression don't run before you can walk?' she asked. Jack thought he could detect a laugh in her voice. 'Seems quite appropriate in this case,' she added looking away from him, 'Don't you think?'

Yes, definitely a laugh in her voice this time, he thought. He scowled. Katherine looked back at him and the barely concealed smile fell from her face.

'Oh, Jack, don't take everything so seriously,' she said, touching his shoulder gently. 'You did really well today, really well, that was a huge step forward. Jack, you went outside, you walked, really walked I mean, all properly and everything.'

Jack was starting to feel a bit better.

'And then,' she continued, 'Jack, you ran, *ran*, I mean, that's huge. And Jack you didn't just run, I mean, crikey, Jack, you even flew today as well!'

She looked at his face and burst out laughing.

Jack looked at her in disbelief; here he was, bleeding, hurting, humiliated, and she was laughing at him, *laughing at him*. He stared at her as she laughed, she was laughing so hard now tears were starting to run down her cheeks. She looked at him and saw the look on his face and tried to stop laughing, but the harder she tried, the more she seemed to find it funny.

Jack was finding it hard now to keep the hurt look on his face; try though he might, Katherine's laughter was becoming infectious, he could feel himself smiling despite trying not to. Though he tried as hard as he could, he could not keep a straight face, he kept smiling and eventually let out a small laugh, which turned into a bigger one and then he was laughing as hard as she was. The pair of them standing in Jack's kitchen, hugging, and laughing so hard they were both crying and it took a long time for the laughter to subside.

9.

The Anny Mall

'Listen, there's somewhere I want to take you on Saturday are you free?' Katherine asked down the phone.

'Yes, what do you have in mind?' asked Jack.

'It's a surprise,' Katherine laughed. 'You'll just have to be patient.' And she hung up the phone.

Saturday dawned bright and sunny. Jack dressed with care in his best jeans and a casual, but smart, shirt. He was looking critically in the mirror at himself, wondering whether he was getting a spot on his cheek, when Pam walked into his room carrying a large pile of freshly washed and ironed clothes.

She watched him for a second, smiling, then she said, 'You look lovely, sweetie. She's a lucky girl.'

Jack whirled around, he had not heard her come in, he had been lost in his own thoughts.

'Thanks, Gran,' he said.

'She's a lovely girl, Jack, and she seems to really like you.' She put the clothes down on his bed and started walking back out of the room, she turned as she got to the door.

'Have a lovely time, darling, I'm off to the shops with Mary. I'll see you later.'

Mary was Pam's closest friend and had been a pillar of strength to her since Alan's death.

'Okay, Gran. Thanks, you have a good time too, see you.'

Pam left the room. Jack looked back at the mirror, a small area of his cheek was red and slightly tender and itchy, he was definitely getting a spot. *Brilliant,* he thought to himself, *just what I need.*

'Where are we going?' Jack asked again, he had asked the same question every five minutes since they had left Katherine's house and started walking down the road in the direction of the town centre.

'How many times do I have to answer this question, Jack?' Katherine asked in mock exasperation. 'Give it a rest.'

'Just give me a clue,' he begged.

She stopped walking and looked at him, her arms folded.

'Brighton,' she said simply.

'Brighton?' Jack repeated questioningly.

'Yes, we need to get the bus.' And she strode off towards the bus stop, not looking back.

He ran after her.

'What's in Brighton?' he asked.

'The place we're going,' she replied and sat on the bench waiting for the bus.

The bus arrived twenty minutes later and they both got on board and sat down together. They chatted while the bus trundled through towns and villages and eventually arrived in Brighton about one and a half hours later. They got off the bus and Katherine started walking towards the seafront. They walked in silence; Jack was desperate to ask again where they were going, but guessed she would not answer. Eventually they came to a small street in the lanes. It was dark, even though the day was sunny, because it was bordered both sides by high walls. Katherine led him down the lane until they came to a grubby green door with peeling paint and a small silver disc embedded in the wood at about eye-level. She turned towards him and smiled.

'We're here,' she announced. 'Jack, this is The Anny Mall, well, that's not its real name. Actually, I don't know if it even has a proper name, but that's what we, when I say 'we', I mean morphers, call it.'

Jack looked at the green door; it did not look very special.

'What's The Anny Mall?' he asked.

'A place for people like us to come and buy stuff,' she replied casually, 'and mix with our own kind. Somewhere we can be ourselves and not have to hide what we are.'

He stared at her and she smiled back at him.

'Ready?' she asked.

'I guess,' he replied a bit nervously.

She turned towards the door and held her left wrist up so that the disc under her skin brushed over the silver disc in the wood, Jack thought he saw a tiny flash of blue light, but it was gone almost as soon as he saw it, and then the door creaked and started opening. Katherine beckoned him to follow and disappeared inside. Jack walked through the door to find himself in a long, and quite dark, tunnel. With a red brick floor and ceiling, and rounded brick walls, it reminded Jack of the Victorian sewers he had seen on the TV, though luckily without the unpleasant smell. Along the walls were intermittent bare light bulbs, most of which were not working and those that were, were not very bright, but there was just enough light to see the way. The tunnel was several hundred feet long and Jack was getting more and more nervous as he stumbled after Katherine towards the ever-brightening light at the end. After a few minutes, they emerged into bright daylight into what looked like a large, Victorian conservatory or greenhouse, with brick walls on all sides and a vast glass ceiling with peeling white, elaborate wrought iron framework that cascaded down from the ceiling in intricate floral patterns. The ceiling looked to be at least four floors high. The main part of the hall was at least the size of an aircraft hangar with what looked like a gap at the far right-hand corner that possibly led to further rooms. The room was crammed with market stalls on either side, but not market stalls like Jack had ever seen before. They were elaborate looking, permanent structures made from metal or glass, some of them even had more than one floor, with spiral staircases winding their way up the sides to allow people to access them. Each one was the at least the size of a small shop, but very open and this allowed the goods on sale to be easily viewed from all angles. They all had names just like shops; some were easy to understand and referred to the owner or the merchandise, like 'Arthur Kip, Ani-Human Designer' or 'Skinassist – Morphing Gadgets', others had long complicated and foreign-sounding names that Jack found hard to say in his head. There were people and animals walking all around them, looking at the things for sale and sitting on wrought iron garden chairs at wrought iron garden tables by the side of stalls that were selling drinks and snacks. Jack was hit by the noise of the buyers and sellers all talking at once, a loud hum that made it hard to hear himself talk. Katherine took his hand and dragged him into the thick of the market.

'This market is only open on Saturdays and Wednesdays, and can only be accessed by an interrupter,' she explained in a loud voice. 'The stalls all sell things for morphers,' she continued, 'Some are unique things just for our kind and some,' she pointed to a shop on the other side of the mall called 'Jim's Cheese', 'can be found in normal shops. There are certain things that come in useful when you change and change back, things that help us find our way and make life a bit easier. Here, look.' She pointed to a stall-come-shop on their left. It was quite small and was only one floor, but had several counters set in a figure of eight pattern so customers could walk around easily. The sign above it said, '*AlterAids*'. Jack looked at the array of products for sale on the first counter; it was covered in objects that he had never seen before and had no idea what they were.

There was a man sitting in the middle of one of the gaps in the counters behind a large wooden writing desk that held a sophisticated till, he was reading a book and drinking a coffee. There were boxes and objects piled several high in the gap in the middle of the other counters.

'Can I help you with something?' the man behind the counter asked, as he looked up from his book.

'No, thanks, we're just looking,' Katherine replied.

'Look at this,' Katherine said to Jack. She picked up what looked like a solid, wide silver bracelet with a tiny silver padlock hanging from it. There were others on the table, some set with jewels and in different metals with patterns engraved on them. Jack, who had been looking around him and had not being paying much attention, suddenly realised the thing Katherine was holding looked exactly like the thing the strange man had brought to his house in the badly wrapped box. Well not exactly the same but near enough, suddenly Katherine had Jack's full attention.

'Hey, I've got one of those!' Jack almost shouted. 'Some strange man came to my house with it, I think mine's really old though.'

Katherine looked at him, surprised.

'It's an interrupter-cuff, you put it around your wrist to protect the interrupter from being stolen from under your skin, you can also get them in other materials, like leather, although, obviously leather is easier to cut.' She was silent for a while, twisting the cuff around in her fingers, then she added, 'Mind you, the Bangers will cut your hand off to get the interrupter, so it's not much of a deterrent.' She placed the silver cuff back on the table.

Jack shivered at the thought of the Bangers cutting hands off, deciding on the spot never to wear his interrupter-cuff, preferring instead to take his chances at just having his skin slit open, should they attack him again!

Next to the cuff on the table was what looked like a dog collar.

'What's this?' Jack asked.

Katherine looked at him and laughed.

'It's a collar,' she said, 'although, perhaps not exactly the same as the usual sort of collars you see.'

She picked the collar up and slipped it around her arm, it immediately shrank to fit her wrist perfectly.

'It's a reflexer; you can wear it all the time. It will always automatically change size to fit around your neck or wherever you wear it, whether human or animal. Like a normal collar, you can put your name and address on it. If you morph into, say, a dog, but before you have the chance to change back you get caught as a suspected stray, if you're wearing a reflexer, they can take you home. Just a bit of a safeguard really.' She added, taking it off her wrist and placing it back on the table. 'Rather expensive and not really that great,' she added in a whisper.

They carried on walking. There were traders selling all sorts of things: tiny purses that could be strapped to the arm or leg so valuables could be kept safe while morphing, mini backpacks that were strapped to the body for storing clothes, and boxes that looked like stones and rocks that could be easily left somewhere outside so human possessions could be found once you had changed back. There were animal clothes shops for those who preferred not to run around naked and on-the-go food pouches. Jack was amazed at all the stuff for sale and at all the people walking around, he'd had no idea there were so many people like him. They stopped at a small refreshment stall that was set to the side and sat outside at a small table.

They both ordered a coffee and Jack sat staring around him in wonder. After about five minutes, the waitress returned with the coffees. She was tall and quite large, she looked middle-aged and had a look that reminded Jack of an angry camel. Jack mused to himself about what sort of morpher she might be.

'Look over there, Jack,' Katherine said, grabbing his arm with one hand and pointing across the room with the other hand.

Jack looked in the direction she was pointing and saw a large black dog trotting along.

'That's Monsley; he lives the whole time as a dog. He only ever becomes human if there is a very good reason to, not many people know what he looks like human. I've heard he lives with an old couple who think he's just a dog; he's lived there so long they keep talking about what they're going to do when he dies, apparently he gets quite upset about it – they seem to planning a long holiday!'

They both laughed and sipped their coffees. Jack looked at the dog again, wondering whether that could have been the dog that saved him from the Bangers in the alleyway. They sat chatting for a little while longer and then they paid their bill and carried on walking.

'Why is this place all under cover, aren't most markets open-air?' Jack asked looking at the high ceiling.

'This isn't most markets,' Katherine laughed. 'Besides, morphing isn't very easy in the rain or snow,' she explained. 'Hair and fur gets wet and becomes sticky and makes changing that much harder. That's why people like coming here they can be themselves and not have to worry about the weather.'

As Katherine spoke, a nervous-looking man approached them from the shadows; he was skinny with very bright blue eyes and several days' stubble on his chin, his clothes were old and tatty and dirty-looking and he looked like he might have been sleeping rough. He lifted a nicotine-stained, shaking hand and waved at Katherine, even though he was only a few feet away. Katherine saw him and smiled.

'Hi, Ski,' she said, happy to see him.

'Hi-ski,' he replied and looked questioningly at Jack.

Katherine followed his gaze and said quickly, 'Oh, Ski this is a friend of mine, Jack. Jack, this is Ski.'

'Hi, pleased to meet you,' said Jack, smiling, but at the back of his mind he was thinking that the man seemed familiar.

Ski stared at Jack and sniffed, after a few seconds he said, 'Hi-ski, pleased to meet you too-ski.'

Jack looked at Katherine who gave him a not-now-I'll-tell-you-later look and she turned back to look at Ski.

'It's good to see you, are you okay?'

Ski looked around, still nervous.

'Okay-ski,' he half whispered, 'Been better-ski, been worse-ski, is your unc-ski here?' 'No, sorry,' Katherine replied. 'Just me and Jack. I think Uncle Leo is at work, catching up on paperwork or something.'

'Too bad-ski,' Ski said. 'Could've done-ski with a word-ski.' And with that, he saluted at both Katherine and Jack and slunk off back into the shadows.

'What? I mean, who was that?' Jack asked staring after him.

Katherine smiled fondly.

'Ski,' she said, 'I'm used to him, but he is quite weird when you first meet him. He's sweet though, good friends with my uncle, they go way back; I think Uncle Leo straightened him out when he got mixed up with drugs or something. Apparently morphing and drugs don't mix, Ski got himself in a mess, though I don't know the details.'

'Why does he put ski on the end of his words?' Jack asked.

'No idea,' said Katherine. 'He's always done it, as long as I've known him anyway.'

'What does he change into?' Jack asked.

Katherine thought for a while.

'Not sure, something like a hedgehog, I think. Uncle Leo says he doesn't morph very often because his eyes are so bright and blue they look very wrong on an animal, besides, growing all those spikes would be very painful.'

They both laughed, then Jack looked thoughtfully at Katherine for a few minutes. The man had seemed familiar, Jack was sure he had seen him somewhere before, he thought about mentioning it, but decided against it.

They spent the rest of the day wandering around and looking at the objects for sale. They met several more of Katherine's friends including a man called Colin, who never used anyone's correct names. They had bumped into him just as they were coming away from a large shop that boasted three floors called 'The Art of Skin', a strange place that sold grotesque paintings of people in the act of morphing whose faces were all twisted in pain.

'Hey, princess!' Colin had called to Katherine in an oily voice.

She had looked at him with slight distaste and said, 'Oh. Hi Colin.' She pointed to Jack, 'This is Jack.'

'Hey, John,' he said without bothering to look in Jack's direction. 'Doc about?' he asked Katherine.

'No,' said Katherine, bluntly.

Colin was gone as quickly as he appeared.

'Why does he do that?' Jack asked slightly annoyed.

'For exactly that reason: he seems to like annoying people,' she gritted her teeth. 'Princess!' she almost spat the word.

At five o'clock Katherine looked at her watch.

'Guess we should be heading for the bus home, though maybe just time for something to eat?' she added, grabbing his hand and pulling him towards a restaurant with two floors that had a balcony that jutted out over the main walkway.

They pushed their way inside the crowded room and

headed for the stairs to the balcony, managing to grab the last empty table. The view was mesmerising, looking down on the people and animals moving around. Jack was able to see a lot further than he could from the ground. While he was looking around him, he spotted a man in the shadow of one of the biggest shops staring up at him. As soon as he caught Jack's eyes the man looked away and started walking quickly to the gap at the end of the hall that Jack had noticed when they first came in, he disappeared down it with one last backward glance at Jack. Wondering where it led, and if there were other rooms to this market, he asked Katherine. She looked in the direction he was pointing.

'Oh, no. I think that leads to offices and storerooms or something,' she said.

They ate pizza and salad and drank Cokes while talking about the things they had seen and the people they had met. Katherine laughed when Jack started adding ski onto the ends of all his words, yes-ski, no-ski, okay-ski, but emitted a pretend, but still quite threatening low growl when he called her princess!

'Are there other places like this?' Jack asked as he finished the last spoonful of his ice cream.

Katherine shrugged.

'Dunno. I've never been anywhere else like this, but then I s'pose I don't need to, everything you could possibly need is here.' She spread her arms out as if to prove her point.

As the ceiling showed, it had started to get dark outside. They made their way back out the restaurant and towards the tunnel. With the fading light, the bare light bulbs seemed to be doing a worse job than before and Jack wondered if more of them had gone out. As they stepped out the grubby green door, it was almost dark. They started walking towards the bus stop and Jack once again had the uneasy feeling they were being watched. He looked into the dark shadows surrounding them, but could not see anything. Looking behind him he saw someone slipping out of the green door and into the darkness and he felt his pulse quicken. *Ridiculous*, he thought to himself, *so what if someone had come out of the door, there had been plenty of people inside the mall; some were bound to be leaving, were they not?* Nevertheless, he took a slightly tighter grip of Katherine's arm and started walking a lot faster to the bus.

Once he had seen Katherine safely home, Jack went the long way to the bus stop and caught his bus home. Sitting staring out the window into the darkness, he thought about the day he had just had. The Anny Mall had been one of the most interesting places he had ever been. He could never have imagined such places existed. But, for all the excitement and interest, he had he also found the place to be slightly sinister with its dark corners and weird characters. Getting off the bus, he walked the few minutes' walk to home, let himself in and went straight to his room. As he entered his room he was shocked to see it had been ransacked, not that he was particularly tidy usually, but now his room was a complete mess. The window was wide open; *obviously where whoever had done this had got in,* Jack thought. Drawers were left open and the contents spilled over the floor. The wardrobe doors were open and the clothes inside hanging off the hangers or left in a heap on the floor. Jack was just wondering who or what had done this when he heard a noise, a scratchy noise that sounded like fingernails walking across a wooden table. He looked towards the direction of the noise and was surprised to see a bird. A very large black bird, but still a bird. The bird stopped walking and looked him straight in the face. It had weird, spooky eyes: one was dark brown, but the other was half dark brown and half bright green. It blinked a couple of times and then took flight; it flew once around the room and then straight out the open window. Jack stared after it, unable to see anything through the darkness, but he remained staring at the place the bird had disappeared from. What on earth had the bird being doing here? Had it been looking for something? What? What could he possibly have that someone or something could possibly want? Unable to think of anything he did his best to tidy up a bit and then sank into bed. As he lay there in the dark, wide awake, something that had been bugging him suddenly came to him: he remembered the strange man who had brought the interrupter cuff to him and realised that it was where he knew that man from the Anny Mall from – Ski. It had been he who had come to his house that evening and given him that badly wrapped package, he had even signed a piece of paper with his name, Ski. And yet there had been no spark of recognition from Ski when he had seen Jack. Temporarily, the bird was driven from his mind.

10.

KATHERINE'S STORY

'Tell me about you,' Jack said.

He and Katherine were sitting on a park bench in the weak sunshine, eating chips out of paper cups and watching the ducks on the pond. It was few days after their trip to the Anny Mall. Jack had told Katherine all about his room being searched, the spooky-eyed bird and the fact that he had realised it had been Ski who had delivered the package that had contained the interrupter-cuff, but Katherine had not understood any of it any better than Jack had. She had said that Ski was a strange man; she liked him, but many found him creepy and more than a bit unreliable. As to why he would give Jack a present, she had no idea. And as for a bird ransacking his room, most likely looking for something, she could not shed any light there either. She could only agree that it was very mysterious.

'Nothing to tell,' Katherine answered. 'I haven't done much.'

'You started morphing into a cat when you were a baby. I'd say that's doing something,' Jack laughed. 'A much more interesting story than most people our age, I'll bet.'

She looked at him and smiled.

'Okay, but if you get bored you only have yourself to blame.

I was born in France on November 7th 1991. I was christened Katherine Felix. No middle name, though I think you know me quite well as Poppy,' she smiled at him and continued, 'my parents were very worried about me when I was born; I was very tiny and covered in fur. Well, when I say worried, I mean appalled, really. They were horrified that I looked like some sort of animal.' She looked sad and Jack put his free arm around her.

'Obviously I don't remember any of this; it's what Uncle Leo has told me. They were so upset, even though the fur did disappear after a couple of days, though apparently it did reappear every so often, that my mother wanted me put me up for adoption.'

Now it was Jack's turn to be horrified.

'She what?' he demanded.

'Don't be too hard on her; neither of them were morphers, they had no idea what was wrong with me. I mean, come on, a furry baby? That's enough to freak anyone out. My mother was a very proud woman, she had been a successful model and had been upset enough to find she was pregnant and that her body would suffer for it, let alone to find out she had given birth to a freak. My father was weak and devoted to my mother; anything she wanted he got for her. He didn't want to give me up, but knew it would be a losing battle with my mother. He secretly contacted my mother's brother, my Uncle Leo, because he was a doctor, hoping he might be able to cure me or something. As soon as Uncle Leo heard my symptoms, he realised exactly what it meant. My father told my mother the adoption people were coming to collect me, knowing she would go out 'to avoid any unpleasantness' and instead Uncle Leo came and whisked me off to England.'

Katherine stared at the pond.

'I've never seen either of them to this day. As far as I know, they still live in France, because, according to Uncle Leo, my mother thinks it's 'chic'. As she said the last word, Katherine raised both her arms and used the index and middle fingers on both her hands to form invisible inverted commas in the air.

'My father used to send money to Uncle Leo, but that soon stopped. I could have brothers and sisters for all I know.'

Katherine looked at Jack and smiled weakly.

'So, Uncle Leo and Auntie Rose became my new parents. All this and I was still only a few days old, as far as I was concerned, they were my parents, though they brought me up to call them Uncle and Auntie. Auntie Rose died when I was only three: cancer,' she added sadly. 'I don't remember her very well, she wasn't a morpher, but obviously she knew about Uncle Leo, so was not easily shocked. Uncle Leo devoted his life to me, he never remarried or even came close; he spent all his time looking after me, teaching me, keeping me safe. He's a wonderful man, you know, Jack,' she added.

'I know,' said Jack.

'Although I was born with fur and it did keep coming back every couple of weeks or so, that was my only symptom of morphing until I was just over a year old, at which time I started changing body parts, much like you started. A leg, then an arm, you know. By the time I was two, I could change completely into the cat you so caringly named Poppy. Morphing at such a young age doesn't come without its own set of problems, you know. I didn't know it was a rare gift, I thought everyone could do it. Plus, at that age you can't control your emotions; every time I got upset or over-happy, bang, I would morph. That was okay if we were at home, but when you're out in public it's not such a good idea. Uncle Leo knew I wouldn't be able to attend normal school, well, you can see how that would look. Someone runs past me in the playground and accidently pushes me over and before you know it all the other kids are crying because they just saw me change into a cat! So he took the decision to school me himself at home. It was easy for him to come up with a reasonable medical condition that would prevent me attending normal school and then he put his career on hold while he turned his efforts to me.'

She had a faraway look in her eyes as she remembered her early days.

'He was a great teacher, Jack,' she continued as she turned to look at him.

'Although, to be honest, it wasn't all maths and English he taught me. He taught me everything he knew about morphing and morphers and my education was very thorough. He told me it was very important that people didn't find out about my special gift, as he liked to call it, that people who couldn't do what I could do just wouldn't understand and might try to take me away. That I had to keep it secret and that I could only 'kitty-switch', as he referred to it then, when I was at home with him. As a kid, you believe what you're told a lot more easily than when you're an adult, so I just accepted everything he told me and lived accordingly.

'At the age of eleven Uncle Leo decided I could be trusted to go to normal school; he spent a lot of time trying to decide which school would be best and finally narrowed it down to two, East Green and Freshfield. Well, obviously, he knew you would be attending East Green and decided it was best for us not to meet yet and so sent me to Freshfield.'

'Why didn't he want us to meet then?' Jack asked.

'I don't know,' Katherine said thoughtfully, 'I suppose he thought I might freak you out or something, you didn't know what you were, so I might have let things slip and...' she trailed off, 'I don't know, but that was the decision he made.'

Katherine fell silent for a while and they both ate their chips and stared at the ducks, though Jack was not really seeing them, he was thinking about what it must have been like to grow up as a morpher, and the opportunities that must have presented to Katherine.

'It must have been great being able to change into a cat any time you wanted, you could just slip away any time you liked,' Jack said.

She looked at him.

'Yeah sort of,' she replied. 'The thing was, Uncle Leo kept a very close eye on me. He knew just how easily and quickly I could change, so he kept me on a very tight lead. Obviously, being a monoskin and only being able to change into a very large elephant, Uncle Leo was not very familiar with how easy it was to get into tiny spaces and hide or even escape. I had only ever changed into Poppy at home, Uncle Leo refused to even let me go out in the garden when I was in my cat form, so I was desperate to get outside and stretch my paws.'

They both smiled at each other at her last comment.

'One day, when I was about nine, I saw my chance. Uncle Leo was busy with a delivery man, who had delivered the wrong thing, and they were in the living room going through the paperwork. The delivery man had left the front door open just a crack, but it was enough. I quickly morphed into Poppy and ran out the door. It was wonderful; do you know, most people don't even notice a cat walking down the street? As a nine-year-old girl, everyone would have noticed me on my own; most people would have wondered where my parents were, but, as a cat, I am almost invisible. You get the odd person who wants to stop and stroke you, which I have to admit is a quite weird experience, how people think they can just touch you, but apart from that, I was free to do whatever I wanted. The outside is quite different to being inside, as you are aware: you smell such amazing smells like grass and trees and other animals and birds, petrol from cars, ladies perfume and lots of foodie smells. And, as you know, you also hear such amazing sounds; everything seems amplified, not just louder, but much, much clearer. As a human, sometimes there are too many sounds all at once that it's hard to distinguish between them, but, as Poppy, I could hear each individual sound very clearly. As we all know, animals hearing and sense of smell is much better than humans, so that's not really surprising, but for me it was a whole new world. I just walked and walked, taking in each new sound or smell, far too wrapped up in what I was doing to notice where I was going.

'I have no idea how long I walked around for, but I didn't realise I'd been gone for such a long time until I noticed it was starting to get dark. I turned around, thinking I should head home and realised I was completely lost. I started to panic; I had never been outside on my own during the day, let alone at night. I decided I was definitely better off staying as a cat and trying to find my way home than if I changed back into a little girl. I wandered around, probably getting more lost, when I eventually came to a place that had a lot of wonderful animal smells and which made me feel safer, so I went inside. At first I had no idea what it was, but found out quite quickly it was a vet's surgery. I found an open door and went inside to find cages of animals all up quite high on tables. Fascinated, I wandered around smelling each new scent. All the animals seemed very interested in me too, they watched me as I walked past, they purred or whimpered, but it all felt quite friendly. I wasn't concentrating on anything but the animals so I never noticed a door open and someone enter the room until I was suddenly whisked up into someone's arms.

'"Hey kitty, where'd you come from?" a female voice had asked, "You don't look sick or injured, and I can't see any empty cages that should be full, so I don't think you've escaped, so where did you come from, hey? I guess I should just pop you in here until I know what to do with you."

'And with that, I was pushed into a tiny, wired cage and the door was locked. Inside the cage was an old blanket, which was clean, but had lingering animal smells. I sat down and stared out of my prison, the woman smiled at me and left the

DEBBIE HOOD

room. Well, you can imagine that was not a good situation to be in, I didn't know what to do. I could hear the woman in the other room telling someone she had found a cat and put it in one of the cages for safe-keeping. I looked around; all the other animals were still watching me with interest, especially a dog in one of the end cages, he didn't look sick like the others did. He didn't have any bandages and he wasn't on a drip, he just kept staring at me, sort of wagging his tail. The woman came back with two plastic bowls; one full of water and the other with some foul-smelling brown stuff, which I assume was cat food. She opened the door to my cage and pushed both bowls inside and then she quickly shut the door again.

"'Well, kitty,' she said, "it's too late to find out who you belong to tonight, so we'll just have to keep you here until the morning."

And that was it, I was locked in for the night. I didn't know what to do, I was so scared Jack. I knew Uncle Leo would be going crazy wondering where I was but there was nothing I could do. There was no room in that tiny cage to change back into a human and I'm pretty sure I wouldn't have been able to escape the building anyway. So I just sat there, crying inside.'

Katherine was quiet for a moment then added, 'By the way, in case you were wondering, cat food is disgusting and from what I've heard, so is dog food so I wouldn't bother trying it if I were you.' She said this with a look of disgust.

Jack laughed, 'It wasn't on my list,' he said.

There was silence for a moment.

'So what did you do?' Jack asked.

'Nothing, what could I do? I lay down and tried to sleep, but my mind just wouldn't close down. I was so scared; I didn't know what was going to happen to me. I was so cross with myself for getting into such a terrible situation that I made a promise that, if I ever got out of there, I would never do anything to disobey Uncle Leo ever again. Even the sounds of the other animals sleeping or whining, which had sounded so friendly when I had first arrived, now made me uneasy. What if I never got home, what if I was stuck as a cat in a cage forever? I tell you, it was a hard lesson. Anyway, I must have fallen asleep eventually, though I don't know how, because I woke in the morning to find the woman was back.

"'Not hungry?" she asked, looking at my food bowl. "Or just missing your owner? Never mind, I'm sure we'll find him or her soon.'

And she was gone again.

Then, I noticed the dog from last night, the one who had stared at me, was missing – his cage was empty. I wondered whether he had been taken away for an operation or something and that made me panic even more. What if I was mistaken for another cat who needed an operation? What if I was operated on when there was nothing wrong with me? What if they removed my interrupter during the operation? I tell you, I was in such a state. I was pacing up and down in my cage, wondering how I was going to get out of this when the woman came back in the room. At first this made me panic even more, though I wouldn't have thought that was possible. Someone entered the room behind her and, to my great relief, I realised it was Uncle Leo.

Uncle Leo came over to my cage and stared through the wire at me.

"'Yes, yes," he cried, "That's my cat. I've been so worried, she's never been out all night before. Thank you, thank you so much for keeping her safe."

Well, the woman gave Uncle Leo a lecture on how to look after a cat, which he took very well, all things considered. I was cringing as I listened to it, knowing every word she said would make it worse for me when I got home. When at last she finished, I was put into a travelling basket and taken home.

Well, you can imagine I was in a lot of trouble. Uncle Leo let me out of the basket and demanded I morph to human, which I did. Then he shouted and ranted at me for at least ten minutes, telling me he'd been up all night worried sick about where I was and what had happened to me, how he had thought about phoning the police but couldn't without a lot of explanation. How he was terrified the Bangers might have got me. How could I be so irresponsible as to just wander off and so on. When eventually he finished shouting, he looked at me with tears in his eyes.

"'Katherine I was so worried," he said, "I thought I'd lost you."

Then he hugged me and said that it was a good job Monsley had been ill, otherwise he might never have found me.'

'Monsley?' asked Jack, though the name sounded vaguely familiar.

'The dog who had stared at me the night before; he had been a morpher, brought in by his 'owners' because he had seemed 'a bit peaky'. Hang on, you've seen him, at the Anny Mall, remember? He lives as a dog most of the time, I told you?'

Jack thought back to the big black dog they had seen at the Anny Mall, the one he had looked at wondering whether it had been him that has saved Jack from the Bangers in the alley way.

'Yes, I remember,' he said.

'Well, he had recognised me for what I was,' Katherine continued,

'It's the eyes, you know, and as soon as he had been released in the morning, he had raised the alarm.

Well, if I thought Uncle Leo kept me on a tight rein before that, that was nothing to the rein he kept me on after that. He never left my side, he even had me chipped.' Katherine said, looking embarrassed and humiliated.

'Chipped?' Jack asked, looking down at what was left of his now cold chips.

Katherine followed his gaze.

'Not that sort of chip,' she laughed. 'You know, a computerised chip, like they do to cats and dogs. They insert a chip just under the skin at the scruff of the neck which can be read to reveal the owners name and address in case the animal ever gets lost.'

'You have one of those?' Jack asked incredulously.

Katherine lifted her hair off the back of her neck and turned her back to Jack.

'Just here,' she said, pointing to her neck.

Jack looked closely and could just make out a tiny lump below her hairline. She let her hair drop.

'Honestly, branded like an animal...' she said, 'you can imagine I was not happy about it, but I had no choice. Uncle Leo said he couldn't trust me and I had to have it done.'

She looked down still embarrassed.

'Not such a bad idea, really,' Jack said, trying to make her feel better. 'I mean, he only had your best interests at heart, didn't he?'

She looked up at him, 'Like it, would you, if he did it to you?' she asked.

Jack shrugged. No, he would not like it, if truth be told. Having that interrupter disc under his skin was irritating enough.

'Anyway,' she continued, 'I have the chip, like it or not. Actually, I've never needed it; Uncle Leo never let me out of his sight after my little vet adventure. Straight home after school every day, never allowed to join any after school clubs or go to friends' houses. I suppose it was my fault, I did give him reason to not trust me, but still, he could have given me a second chance.'

'Is that why you always kept to yourself at school?' Jack asked.

'Yes and no. I've always been a bit of a loner anyway,' she answered. 'I was always hoping I would meet someone like me, like us,' she corrected, 'you know, another morpher, someone I could be myself with, someone I could be Poppy with. But the only morphers Uncle Leo introduced me to were adults, until you, of course,' she added brightly.

'Now that was when my life suddenly became more fun,' she went on happily. 'One day Uncle Leo said he had an important job for me, he wanted me to keep an eye on someone, a very special someone. He said it was important that I befriend this person as a cat and report back if I suspected any morphing activity. Uncle Leo was working on the theory that you wouldn't try to hide any changes from a cat. I was excited, I would get to go outside and have a bit of fun. We went through exactly what Uncle Leo wanted me to do. Get into your garden while you were there and sniff around a bit, pretend to be interested in the flower smells, stare at you with my strange cat eyes so you would remember me and then leave. The following day, I was to do the same again and the next day and so on, until, eventually, I let you stroke me and then we became friends.'

Jack smiled, remembering meeting Poppy, how happy that little cat had made him when he had no other friends.

'Uncle Leo drove me to your house and dropped me by your garden fence; he wasn't happy about letting me out of his sight, but he knew he would have to or it wouldn't work,' she continued. 'I jumped over the fence and there you were, you know the rest, as soon as I jumped back over the fence I got back in the car and Uncle Leo drove me home.' She had a faraway look in her eyes again.

'Those were my favourite days, Jack,' she said, looking at him. 'Spending time with you, I loved it when you started calling me Poppy, it was so sweet.'

Jack blushed, 'Bit silly,' he mumbled, embarrassed.

'No,' she insisted, 'I liked it, to me it meant you liked me, if you cared enough to name me. Anyway, I loved those days, I got out the house and away from Uncle Leo's stare, but not just that, I loved spending time with you. I wished I could tell you the truth, you know, be myself, but I couldn't. You were my only friend, Jack, I was longing to see you do some sort of morphing, I was longing to see for myself that you were a morpher and therefore I could tell you who I was.'

'I didn't know,' said Jack, 'I wish I had, it would have been great to have someone to share all those weird things with; I was scared, I thought I was losing my mind.'

Katherine looked at him sadly.

'I know,' she said. 'Thinking about it now, we didn't do things the right way, I should have told you who, or rather what, I was but Uncle Leo didn't want you involved in our world if you didn't belong here. If the operation had stopped the morphing process or something it would have been cruel to get your hopes up, or scare the hell out of you, whichever way you look at it,' she laughed. 'Besides, we don't shout about what we can do, we keep it to ourselves and, if you weren't one of us...' she trailed off.

'Why do you keep it secret?' Jack asked. 'Are you ashamed or something?'

'Of course not,' she replied indignantly, 'on the contrary really, most of us are very proud of what we are and what we can do. It's just that, well, others may not understand. People like to think they're broad-minded, but the days of believing in mythical creatures are long gone. Vampires, witches, mermaids, you know the sort of things, no one believes in those anymore.'

'Are you saying there are such things as vampires, witches and mermaids?' Jack asked astounded.

She looked at him and laughed, 'I don't know,' she said. 'As a morpher, I know morphers exist, but I have no idea about the others, maybe, maybe not.'

Jack had looked confused at this answer so Katherine elaborated.

'Look, if we as morphers don't tell anyone else of our existence, except other morphers, because we don't want to be used as circus freaks or experimented on, or whatever they would do to us if they found out. Then I guess if there are others out there with...' she faltered over the word but eventually settled for, '*Secrets*, and they also wanted to keep it from anyone but their own type, well, we wouldn't know would we?'

She was quiet for a moment and then added, 'It's a bit like believing in aliens I suppose, you know, life on other planets. You don't see any proof, but you find it hard to believe you're the only ones. I guess we'll never really know for sure.'

They were quiet for a few minutes then Jack said, 'S'pose we should make a move.'

They got up and slowly started walking towards the park exit. When they came to a bin, they threw away the paper cups that had held their chips.

As they walked, Jack asked, 'So why did your uncle change his mind and move you to my school?'

Katherine stopped walking for a moment, then carried on, saying, 'I don't know, I never asked him. I was so glad to be moving nearer to you I never thought about Uncle Leo's reasons. I bet he didn't expect this though,' she said, kissing his cheek and then skipping off in front of him. Jack quickened his pace to keep up with her.

They walked in silence for a few minutes, and then Jack said, 'Would you want to see them again, your parents I mean?'

Katherine stopped walking and looked at him, then she looked down at the ground, after a few seconds she said, 'Why?' Then, looking back up at him, 'Why would I want to? I mean, I have people who love me, care what happens to me, why would I want to see the people who gave me away?'

'Sorry,' Jack said, 'stupid question.'

'No it wasn't,' she insisted, 'it wasn't a stupid question at all. I just don't need them in my life, Jack. Let's say I did meet them, and they acted just the way they did when I was a baby;

they were horrified and disgusted at me, that would just hurt, Jack. But then on the other hand, let's say I met them and they liked me, then I'd be angry that they gave me away and never gave me a chance, plus then I'd feel guilty if I liked them because I'd feel like I was being ungrateful to Uncle Leo, who took me in, looked after me, loved me.'

She was silent for a while, looking around. Then she looked back at Jack and, smiling, said, 'Anyway, it's not about to happen. Besides, they could be dead for all I know!'

'Like mine,' said Jack. 'Well, my Mum. I don't even know who my Dad was, or maybe, is.'

'Right,' she said putting her arm through his and starting them walking again, 'no more talk of parents, agreed?'

'Agreed,' said Jack, and they fell in to step with each other. After a few minutes walking in silence, Jack said, 'So, you were wrong, you know.'

'What?' asked Katherine, as she stopped walking and stared at him. 'When? When was I wrong?'

'When you said there was nothing to tell, that you haven't done much.' Jack said, 'sounds to me as though your life has been pretty interesting so far.'

Katherine smiled; she took Jack's hand and started walking again, 'Not as interesting as I hope it's going to get,' she said, smiling.

11.

KATHERINE'S DISAPPEARANCE

The sun was shining and it was just too inviting to stay indoors. Prince was walking down the road on his own. Jack had just left his house after being caught by his gran. Thinking his gran had gone shopping, Jack had morphed into Prince in the kitchen, carefully leaving the door open and a key and some clothes behind large plant pot so he could get back in. His gran had walked into the kitchen and found the tailless dog standing in the middle of the room.

'Get out of here,' she had shouted at him, taking him by surprise and making him jump. He had run out the door and she had run after him, slamming the door behind him. He had stopped outside the door for just a few seconds, his heart pounding, thinking how lucky it was that the morphing process had been completed before she had caught him, then he had taken off at a run to get away as quickly as possible. It had been a close call and he would have to be careful in future that it did not happen again. There would be too many questions that he could not answer if his gran caught him midway between human and dog.

Now he was headed for the park, wanting nothing else but to feel the grass beneath his paws.

It was Prince's first venture outside without Poppy and although he felt nervous, he also felt excited. He knew he was more conspicuous than Poppy; cats were always wandering around outside on their own, dogs were usually accompanied by owners and quite often on leads, but he was sure that once he got to the field no one would notice him.

The field was as wonderful as it had been the first time; the cool grass, which was soft and springy, was the perfect running surface and Prince ran and jumped and generally frolicked around for at least an hour. He had a wonderful time and even though he had been running for quite a while, he was not even out of breath. Thinking he might be pushing his luck by staying out too long, though also a bit worried he would bump into his gran again if he went home too soon, he began a very slow saunter across the field towards home. Not really looking where he was going, he was surprised to see feet coming towards him, three pairs of feet, in fact, looking very much like feet that belonged to men. Looking up Jack's surprise turned to horror when he looked straight into the face of Eric Tarver who was grinning evilly. Jack knew that grin of old; it was the look that said Eric had found a victim and he was staring right at Prince.

'Well, will you look at what we've got here,' Eric said, not taking his eyes off Prince. 'What on earth is it?' he asked in a sort of disgusted tone. 'It's sort of like a dog, but not a whole one. Where's your tail, you stupid mutt?' he said the last bit loudly and slowly as though he was talking to someone a bit slow.

Matt and Danny who were standing behind him sniggered. Seemingly encouraged by their response Eric moved forward towards Prince.

'Well, mutant,' he continued, 'what's wrong? Cat got your tongue?' He laughed loudly at his own joke, and both Matt and Danny laughed as well.

Jack was scared, he had not been face to face with Eric for

a long time and he had forgotten just how horrible he was. Backing away slightly, he was just wondering to himself whether he would be able to out run them without tripping over his own four feet, when suddenly, Eric lunged at him, throwing both his arms around Prince's neck, causing the surprised dog to fall sideways onto the ground with Eric landing on top of him.

Eric released him and stood up.

'Useless mutt, can't even defend yourself can you?' He spat on the ground. Looking round at his friends he said, 'What shall we do with him?' He looked around the field, 'He doesn't seem to have an owner.'

Jack got back on his four feet, he was seething; picking on kids at school was bad enough, but picking on animals, just for being there, was very low indeed.

Eric looked at him again, thought for a few moments then said to Matt and Danny.

'Come on, let's go. Stupid mutant mutt is boring.' And he started walking off in the opposite direction.

Jack was very relieved; he started walking slowly towards home when, suddenly, he stopped. A voice inside his head told him he was being stupid and he should just go home, but he was angry and feeling a bit reckless after his lone outside adventure. He turned around and started following Eric. He sped up until he caught up with all three of them. Danny noticed him first.

'Hey, Eric, look who's following you. I think he likes you.'

Eric turned around and stared at Prince.

'You really are stupid, aren't you?' he said, almost gleefully. 'Well you're gonna be sorry.' He looked around for something, Jack had no idea what he was looking for and did not care, he walked closer to Eric and Prince started growling. Eric looked back at him in surprise.

'Did you growl at me?' he asked in a mock shocked voice.

Prince growled louder.

'Ooh, you're so scary,' Eric teased.

Prince's growl turned into a snarl, teeth bared and muzzle curled. Eric did not look quite so confident; he looked at Prince and then turned to Matt and Danny and said again, 'Come on, let's go.'

But, as he started walking away, Prince followed him, snarling and snapping his jaws aggressively. Eric turned back and looked at him and this time he had a slightly scared look on his face.

'All right, stupid dog,' he said, 'I'm going,' and he started walking away very quickly.

But Prince was not giving up, he started walking quickly after Eric, still snarling, causing Eric to speed up to a run, so Prince started running. Eric ran faster, Prince ran faster. Jack knew he could run a lot faster than this, he could easily catch and overtake Eric if he wanted to, but this was not a question of how fast he could run, this was question of how fast he could make Eric run.

They ran, Eric looking more and more scared and running at full speed, looking behind him every few seconds to see if the dog was still there. Jack could have carried on for a lot longer, but he decided that was enough, he had made his point. He stopped running, Eric did not – he carried on running. Inside Jack was laughing to himself; it had been so much fun, the running, the snarling, it had felt good.

Walking home Jack felt immensely proud of himself, he had gone out on his own and he had not only stood up to Eric, he had frightened him away. Okay, so he had not frightened Eric away, but Prince had and that was almost the same thing. When he got home he morphed as quickly as he could, grabbed his clothes and the key from behind the flowerpot and let himself in the house, still smiling to himself.

'I wish I'd been there,' Katherine said, 'it was reckless and a bit dangerous, but oh how I wish I'd seen Eric's face.'

'It was good,' Jack said with a faraway look on his face like he was remembering some sweet memory, 'I mean, he looked terrified, really scared. I'm surprised he didn't wet himself.'

They both laughed.

'He deserved it, he's a horrible bully and he deserves a taste of his own medicine.' Katherine continued.

They were sitting in the lounge at Doctor Noah's house playing chess; Jack was winning as he always did, though Katherine was getting better.

'Check,' Jack said.

'Oh no, not again,' said Katherine, getting up and stretching her legs.

'Want another game?' Jack asked.

'No, I'm bored with always losing,' she said smiling. 'How about a game of tennis?'

'I've never played tennis before,' said Jack.

'Good,' said Katherine. 'Then I should win.'

'You need to hit it harder,' Katherine shouted from the other side of the tennis court. 'At least if you ever want it to make it over the net.'

'Ha ha,' said Jack without humour. He was not finding tennis very easy. Running had come very easy to him, considering the life of no exercise he had led before his operation, running had been like second nature to him once he had his new heart. Tennis, on the other hand, was not so easy; you had to run but also use your arm to hit something, the coordination between the running and the hitting was proving to be something of an issue for Jack.

Katherine laughed again as Jack's ball hit his side of the net.

'You need to hit it harder, oh, and higher,' she called.

Ha ha, he said in his head this time. *Okay*, he thought, *you want it harder and higher? Here is comes*, and he belted the ball to other side of the court. Katherine missed it. She had a slightly shocked look on her face.

'Better,' she said in surprised voice. 'Er, much better.'

They had been playing for about half an hour and this was the first time one of the balls Jack had hit had made it over the net. He felt quite proud of himself, like he was finally making progress, but when Katherine sent a ball flying in his direction, although he managed to hit it, it hit the net again.

Jack swore. Katherine laughed as she walked towards the net, 'Don't be so hard on yourself... again.' She added, 'You always think you should be able to do things straight away, without learning them, or practising them.'

She sighed at the hurt look on his face. 'Oh, Jack,' she said. 'Come on, this is the first time you've played tennis. What, you think you should be winning Wimbledon already?'

Jack smiled. Yeah, stupid to get upset really, it was his first time. He just wished he could do something in front of Katherine without making himself look like a fool.

The weather was dry and quite sunny, not such perfect conditions for running around working up a sweat. Jack and Katherine were playing tennis on an outside court that belonged to the local sport centre, it was in the centre grounds, flanked on two sides by a field, one side by the centre building itself and the fourth side backed onto a small wood.

Jack was serving with the sun in his eyes; he hit the ball, then, holding his arm to shield his eyes, he watched it hit the net. He groaned. Walking slowly towards the net to retrieve the ball for the umpteenth time he saw a movement from the corner of his eye. Turning slightly to stare at the woods, as he stopped walking he thought he saw movement again. Squinting and shielding his eyes against the bright glare of the sun, he strained to see into the dark depths of the dense trees. Nothing, no movement.

'What are you looking at?' Katherine called, staring in the same direction as Jack. He looked at her.

'Nothing,' he called back, 'I just thought I saw... nothing.'

Jack picked up the ball and walked back to the edge of the court, he felt slightly uneasy. He had that strange feeling he was being watched, followed, like he'd had at the Anny Mall and in the Hall of Mirrors at the fairground. He looked at the woods again, he could not see any movement, but there were lots of dark places, places that would be easy to hide in and spy on people, places that would keep you concealed if you wanted to do the seeing without being seen.

'What's the matter?' Katherine called, sounding slightly inpatient, 'What are you looking at?'

Jack's head snapped back to look at Katherine.

'Nothing, sorry,' he yelled back at her.

And he raised his arm and hit the ball towards Katherine, this time it made it over the net, but barely. Katherine ran forward and hit it back at Jack. Jack ran and swung his racquet towards the oncoming ball and missed it. As he watched it fly past he trod backwards awkwardly, twisted his ankle and fell over. He swore again and Katherine ran over to him.

'You okay?' she asked as she got nearer, sounding concerned.

'Yeah, I'm fine,' Jack replied. 'A twisted ankle and hurt pride, I'll live.'

'Do you want a rest?' she asked.

'Yeah, for about twenty years I think,' Jack said.

'Not liking tennis?' she asked with a smile in her voice, 'Shocking.'

He looked at her, she was infuriating, always knowing the right thing to say in any situation, always having a go at him for being hard on himself... *Always right*, he thought bitterly. Everything came so easy to her, she had no idea how hard things were for him, or how bad it felt to always get things wrong. Then he looked at her properly, her long tawny blonde hair blowing in the slight breeze, her amazing blue-green eyes shining with un-voiced laughter, her graceful body moving like a ballerina; he could never really be mad with her, he just wished he could do something, anything apart from chess, that would make her proud instead of making her laugh.

They found a bench and sat down, Katherine had two cans of Coke in her bag so they sat in the sun and drank.

After a few minutes Katherine said, 'I saw someone selling ice creams when we came in the park, would you like one?'

The sun was still shining and Jack was quite hot. *An ice cream would be great*, he thought.

'Oh, I'd love one,' he said. 'I'll get them.'

But Katherine was already on her feet, purse in hand.

'No,' she said, skipping away from him. 'I'll go, you rest that ankle.' She was a few feet away when she called back, 'What do you want?'

'Ninety-nine,' Jack answered and with that she quickened her pace walking backwards waving. She reached the edge of the woods, waved again and then disappeared behind the trees.

Jack faced back towards the sun, eyes closed and enjoyed the feeling of the sun on his face. He sat there for a while just relaxing and within a few minutes he had fallen asleep.

Jack woke suddenly, for a few seconds he was not sure where he was; he looked around and remembered being in the park, with Katherine – *Katherine*. He looked around again, he was alone. Katherine who had gone for ice cream and had not yet returned. He looked at his phone, she had been gone for over thirty minutes yet the ice cream stand had only just been behind the woods, about five minutes away. He stood up quickly, shivering even though the sun was still shining, and looked all around.

He called out, 'Kat? Kat are you there?'

Nothing, no response, he called again.

'Kat? Katherine? Where are you?'

Nothing, there was nobody near. Jack looked at his phone and rang Katherine's mobile number. After a few seconds he heard the familiar ringtone of *Born Free* ringing in Katherine's bag, which was still sitting on the bench. She had not taken her phone when she had gone to get the ice creams. He grabbed the bag and started walking quickly in the direction that he had last seen Katherine, calling all the way.

'Kat? Katherine?'

He broke into a run as he reached the edge of the woods, twisted ankle forgotten, still calling. He saw the ice cream stand, the man serving ice creams was still there, but there was no sign of anyone else. He ran towards it.

'Excuse me,' he said as he reached the counter.

'Yes, how can I help you?' the man asked.

'I'm looking for my girlfriend,' Jack said quickly. 'She came here to get ice creams about half an hour ago – small, blonde, blue-green eyes, have you seen her?'

The man thought for a few seconds.

'No, I think I would remember her.'

Jack could feel the panic rising inside him; he felt light-headed, sick, hot and yet, at the same time, shivery. *Where could she be?* He could feel the prickling of fur starting all over his body.

'Not now!' he shouted out loud, making the ice cream man jump.

He looked around again wildly. The panic inside him threatening to boil over, but the prickling subsiding, when his eyes fell on the woods. He stared at the woods, the dark woods, the woods where he had thought he had seen something move, the woods where someone could have been hiding. He ran towards the dark, calling her name. As he entered the cool shade of the trees his voice sounded louder as he called for Katherine. The woods were not big, it only took Jack a few minutes to run their entire length, calling all the time. Nothing. He walked slowly back, peering through the gloom in every direction; there was no sign of anyone or any sort of movement. Then something caught Jack's eye, a glint of something shiny, he ran towards it. There, laying on the ground just inside the wood, was a small, shiny something glinting in the weak sun. Jack picked it up, it was a purse and not just any purse, he had seen this one before, many times: turquoise in colour with small shiny beads in all shades of blue and green – it was Katherine's purse.

Jack lay on his bed in the dark; he had spent nearly four hours searching for Katherine. When he had finally finished combing every square inch of the park and the woods, he had retraced their steps and revisited everywhere they had been that day, but he had not found anything since her purse. She had disappeared, vanished. He was not ashamed to admit he had been crying; he felt useless and stupid. Useless because he could not find her and stupid because he had let her go off without him in the first place. Why had he not gone with her to get the ice creams, his stupid ankle had not been that bad. How could he have just let her go? Why had he not said no to the stupid ice cream in the first place?

He had fought down the morphing that had threatened when the panic set in at the park, but had given in to it once he got home, relishing in the pain that he felt he deserved for letting down the one person who would never let him down. He had fully morphed into Prince and back again three times and was now human again and exhausted. Lying in the dark, he was trying desperately to think of where she could be, but his mind just kept drawing blanks. Just when he thought he would go out of his mind with worry he heard a noise in the darkness, a text message was coming through on his phone. He sat up and reached into his pocket and pulled out his phone, he read the message and his blood ran cold. He jumped to his feet no longer feeling tired, but wide awake, his mind racing. He read it again, dropped the phone on the bed and then ran from the room, grabbing his jacket as he ran. He ran straight downstairs and out the front door, not even bothering to close it behind him. Jack had only one thing on his mind as he ran and that was to get to the alley as quickly as possible, it was his only thought. It was a long way to the alley, he would normally have taken the bus for a distance like that, but the bus was the furthest thing from his mind. The distance seemed nothing at all. As he ran he glanced around, noticing the night landscape, fields, farms and then finally shops as he entered the town. He caught a brief sight of his reflection in the dark shop windows as they flashed past and he was reminded of the dreams he had often had, the running dreams, the dreams where he had been running towards something that was just out of sight. Well, now he knew what it was he had been running to, now he knew what it was that had always remained hidden but he had been desperate to get to: it was Katherine and he was terrified. In what seemed no time at all he had almost reached the alley and he slowed to a walk. He stuffed his hands into his jacket pockets and groaned, only then did he realise that he had left his phone behind. Cursing under his breath, he visualised it, laying on his bed, still flashing the message.

'Here kitty, kitty. Bang.'

12.

The Bangers

Standing at the entrance to the alley, Jack stopped and tried to look into the darkness, but could see nothing. It was a very dark evening, the crescent moon gave very little light and the streetlamps obviously had not been fixed since the last time he was here, when only one had been working and that one could not be seen from where Jack was standing. Jack took several deep breaths; this was very dangerous. He had no idea whether the Bangers would even be here, just because they had been here once did not necessarily mean they would be here again, but it was his only hope, he had absolutely no idea where else to find them. He took a slow, tentative step forward. His heart was thumping and his breathing was very heavy. A little voice in his head warned him that once he started down the alley there was no going back. He took another step forwards; it was now or never.

'Now,' he said to himself and walked into the darkness.

The alley was not only dark, but also very quiet. Jack was very aware of the sound of his own footsteps; he tried to walk without making too much noise, as he did not want to announce his arrival if anyone was there. He walked several steps and then stopped, listening as hard as he could. There was a faint noise coming from the other end of the alley, it was hard to hear even with Jack's extra sensitive hearing, but it sounded like people talking quietly. Jack kept as still and as quiet as he could, straining his ears, but he could not work out what they were saying. 'They' were definitely men, Jack was sure of that, but he could not tell if they were voices he had heard before or not. Just then the wind got up and blew hard down the alley, bringing with it dust and leaves and a whooshing noise. Jack covered his face to avoid dust getting in his eyes. The sound and swirling debris lasted for a few minutes and then settled as quickly as it had picked up. When the silence fell again, Jack took his hands away from his face and could hear the men's voices; this time they sounded much closer and, although he still could not make out what they were saying, they sounded a lot more familiar, one sounded as though he had a cold.

As Jack was standing there listening, he felt something brush past his leg. He jumped and let out a small grunt of surprise, as he looked down he could vaguely see a small animal of some sort running very fast into the darkness in front of him. He stood frozen to the spot, listening intently to the voices, which had suddenly stopped. Silence rang out; there was no sound at all except for the faint whoosh of the wind at the end of the alley. Why had the men stopped talking? Jack strained his ears even more, but could hear nothing. He started walking very slowly forward, keeping his footsteps almost completely silent. His whole body was tense and he had almost stopped breathing altogether. Two more careful steps and suddenly out of the gloom came two figures. Jack felt the tiny animal brush past his leg again, and then a high pitched voice spoke.

'Well, well, well, what has we 'ere?'

The voice rang out in the silent air. Jack froze; he had heard that voice before, in the same alley, when the Bangers had tried to steal his interrupter. It had been dark and he had not seen the man's face, but the voice sent chills down his spine. He looked up slowly and came face to face with a large, imposing-looking man; the high voice did not go with the look of the man at all. The man was bald and had a long scar down one of his cheeks and right then he was looking very pleased with himself.

'Not your day, is it?' the man said, walking slowly towards Jack, 'not your day at all, Jacky.'

Jack felt himself take an involuntary step backwards and bumped into someone behind him. He quickly turned and saw one of the other the men from the alley that night, one of the two men who had called each other Rocket and Kev, one of the two he had seen in the light of the streetlamp. They had done it to him again, penned him in, given him nowhere to escape to.

'Where's Katherine?' he asked, his voice shaking, giving away how frightened he felt, 'what have you done with her?'

'Ah, 'ow touching,' the man called Kev said, 'worried about your little girlfriend, are ya?' He took a step closer to Jack and added, 'You should be. She's somewhere you can't find 'er.'

'If you've hurt her,' Jack started, but the man called Kev started to laugh.

'Oh yeah, what're you gonna to do 'bout it?' he laughed again, 'are you going to hurt me?' he asked in a mock-scared voice.

The others joined in the laughter.

'Come on,' the man with the high voice said. 'We haven't got all day; we need to get back to Vic. You grab the boy, Rocket, and let's get outta here.'

Before the high-pitched voiced man had finished speaking, Jack felt the man called Rocket grab him by the arms and start dragging him towards the road. There was no point in trying to struggle: the man called Rocket may have been skinny, but he was much stronger than Jack. Jack was dragged and pulled along backwards on the rough pavement until they came to an old van, which Jack could just see if he twisted his head as far round to the right as it would go. As they got nearer, the man called Kev opened the back doors. Rocket lifted Jack by his arms, which were behind his back and threw him inside the van. Jack's arms felt as though they had both been dislocated at the shoulders, although as he could still move them he suspected they were just badly bruised. He heard the three men move to the front of the vehicle and open the front doors to get in. Someone had crudely fixed chicken wire between the back of the van where Jack was and the front seats, so there was no escape for Jack via the front doors.

The man with the high-pitched voice shouted sarcastically to Jack over his shoulder, 'Hope you're comfy back there, do let us know if you need anything, won't you.'

The three men all laughed, Jack ignored them, he looked around the van; there was nothing in the back except a spare tyre, some old rusty tools and a tarpaulin. Certainly with the doors locked and the chicken wire there was no escape.

The van started moving and Jack was thrown across the floor. He sat up, still rubbing his sore shoulders. It was not a good situation; even though he had purposely gone to the alley in the hope of finding one of the Bangers to try to find out where Katherine was, he had been so angry and wound up and scared he had not thought this through, he had not thought about what he would do if he found one, let alone three! Now he was helpless in the back of a van with three men who, from what he had heard about them, could kill him at any moment for no particular reason. Last time he had met them they had been intent on stealing his disc, this time they seemed to have no interest in it at all, why? With his left hand, he absentmindedly started rubbing the area where the smaller, newer, back-up disc was, the one that Dr Noah had insisted on inserting under the skin of his right wrist after that last attack. Dr Noah had been right, you could not see the disc through the skin; it made him feel safer, but did nothing to make him feel less frightened.

The van travelled for what felt to Jack like hours. The men in the front did not say much; they put the radio on full volume and sang along tunelessly to any song they remotely knew, even if they had to make the words up. Jack took little notice, he was still trying to make sense of his situation. It was difficult because he really was not even sure what his situation was. Okay, so he knew he was in the back of a van with three Bangers in the front and they were taking him somewhere, but where and why? He was no further to finding out what had happened to Katherine, or where she was or anything. He could not help feeling cross with himself, it was one thing to act the hero, but if you are going to do that sort of thing you really need to plan. And plan, well, he had not planned at all. He remembered something one of his schoolteachers had said to his class once when they had been revising for an exam. The teacher was trying to impress on the class how much revising they needed to do.

'You cannot revise too much,' he had said. 'Just remember: if you fail to prepare, you prepare to fail.'

Well, lessons are best learned when you live them; he had certainly not prepared and now he had certainly failed.

The van hit a bump in the road and Jack was thrown onto his side, he heard a cruel laugh from the front and assumed one of the men had either seen or heard him fall over. He tried to ignore them. He sat up and wondered how much longer the journey would be. After what seemed like several hours, though in reality Jack suspected it was probably only an hour or two, the van pulled into a petrol station. Jack watched as the man who had been driving jumped lightly out of the van and filled up with petrol, he then walked into the shop presumably to pay. After a few minutes the shop door opened and a strange man walked through it and towards the van, he got in, started the engine and drove onto the road. Jack was shocked that a completely different man had got in the van and started driving and the other two men did not even acknowledge him. Even if they did know him and were expecting him to join them, it was still strange they did not even say hello. The man with the high voice, bald head and facial scar had been driving, this man was shorter and thinner than the previous driver with wispy ginger hair and full, straggly ginger beard. Jack only gave this a few minutes thought, however; it made no difference to his situation who the Bangers were.

They drove further and further, it felt to Jack like the middle of the night. There was no way he could have slept, however, even if he had not been so scared and his mind racing, every time they hit a bump in the road or swerved to miss something, Jack was thrown onto the floor. The bumps and swerves happened a lot and Jack suspected either the driver was not very good or it was being done on purpose to make him as uncomfortable as possible. As the sky was starting to lighten, indicating dawn was about to break, Jack looked towards the front of the van and noticed the original driver was back in the driving seat; his bald head was catching the early morning light and his scar was just visible from where Jack sat. *Odd*, he thought. He did not remember the van stopping again since the petrol station and was sure he had not been sleeping. A few minutes later the van pulled into a service station, all three men got out and locked the van before walking into the building. Jack was left alone, locked in the van. His situation, although changed slightly, had not improved much. What Jack guessed to be about an hour later, the three men returned. Two climbed in the front while the third opened the back doors and threw a cheese sandwich and a bottle of water at Jack, then he closed the doors and went round to get in the front with the others. Jack looked at the food and water, he had to admit he was hungry and thirsty, so he grabbed them both from the floor and began to eat and drink. The men laughed and Jack wondered if they had done something to the food. Deciding he was too hungry to care and that he might need his strength later, he finished the sandwich and the water.

When the sun was overhead, Jack guessed it was about midday; he vowed to himself never to leave the house again without his phone, it was stupid to have left it behind, although he was pretty sure the Bangers would have taken it if he'd had it with him, after all they knew the number so it would not have been hard to ring it. He was beginning to think this journey would never end when the van suddenly turned left onto a very long gravel drive. They waited as the ornate, cast iron electric gates slowly opened, and, as they drove through, Jack noticed a large, polished brass plaque that read:

'Jackson Hall, Private, Keep Out.'

Crunching along quite slowly on gravel, they passed woods on either side; the drive went on for at least half a mile before it opened up onto a magnificent garden. On the left there was a huge ornamental pond with a brick bridge over the centre, surrounded by a manicured lawn with carefully chosen plants all in pale pink. Ducks and geese swam lazily in the sunshine, whilst being watched by a huge black cat sitting on an ornamental stone bench. The cat looked up and watched them as they passed before it looked back at the pond. On the right was a hedge maze, quite large in size but the trees were not very tall so, although a small child could get lost, an adult could easily see over the top to find their way out. Jack wondered whether it was still growing and would therefore get taller. *Kind of pointless otherwise*, he thought. The drive bent round the right and the house came into sight. It was a huge Georgian mansion with large concrete pillars flanking the double front doors. It was painted white, which seemed to almost shine in the sun. The long windows, of which there were too many to easily count, looked imposing with their glinting glass that allowed no clue as to what lay behind them. The van pulled up in front of the doors and the three men climbed out. Jack's heart started pounding as he heard the back doors being unlocked. One of the men climbed in and grabbed him roughly, pushing him towards the exit. Jack stumbled onto the ground, but did not fall over; the man jumped out behind him and pushed him towards the house. The other men were already at the door, knocking. After a few seconds the door opened and the two men disappeared inside. The man behind Jack pushed him again and Jack started walking towards the door with a feeling of impending doom. He climbed the four steps and walked as confidently as he could. After the bright sunshine outside, the inside of the house looked very dark, Jack crossed the threshold into the gloom beyond.

13.

Jackson Hall

As soon as he walked through the door into the dark interior, Jack could smell the familiar sweet scent that he knew belonged to Katherine; knowing she must be somewhere in this giant house gave him added confidence, something he desperately needed. As his eyes adjusted to the gloom he looked around, the house was very grand. The hall was huge, at least as large as a swimming pool, with an enormous curved, ornamental staircase winding around the far wall. The floor was marble, which Jack was finding hard to walk on because the man behind him kept pushing him forwards and this caused Jack's feet to slip on the polished surface. The walls were covered in large paintings and wall hangings, which, given the grandness of the house, Jack assumed they were probably priceless works of art. There was very little furniture in the hall; a large, intricately woven rug in the middle and a small gold table to the left that held an enormous vase of flowers, were the only things that were on the floor.

One of the men in front of Jack called out into the seeming emptiness, 'Vic, we're back!'

There was no answer, so he called again.

'Hey Vic, you 'ere?'

Still no answer, he turned to the man behind Jack.

'Rocket, take the kid upstairs. I'll find Vic.' And with that, he turned and disappeared through a large door to the left.

'You 'eard, up the stairs.' the man called Rocket said to Jack, giving him another shove forwards.

Jack started forwards towards the stairs, his feeling of extra confidence leaving him almost as fast as it had arrived. Going upstairs seemed like a bad idea to Jack, as it made it impossible to make a run for it, should the occasion arise. As he started climbing the stairs he noticed the sweet fragrance he associated with Katherine getting stronger with every step and this helped to calm him slightly; wherever she was, he was getting nearer to her. At the top of the stairs the man behind Jack grunted for him to turn right, after several feet down a very sumptuous landing that was carpeted in a very new, light beige carpet and furnished with what looked to Jack like antique occasional tables and chairs, Jack was shoved through a door on his left. He fell inside the room, lost his balance and, as he put his arms out in front of himself to break the fall, he noticed someone else was already in the room standing on the other side by the large bay window.

'Kat,' he almost shouted as he landed badly on his left arm; he heard the faint click of the door being locked behind him.

Scrambling to his feet he saw her running towards him, she flung her arms around his neck and clung to him, sobbing.

'Are you okay?' he asked her.

She pulled away slightly to look at him.

'Yes,' she said in small voice, 'I'm okay, but oh, Jack. I've been so scared.'

'Have they hurt you,' he asked, almost afraid of the answer.

'No,' she replied, 'but they've been really horrible to me, telling me all the awful things they would do to me if you didn't come to rescue me...' she trailed off. She looked into his eyes, 'Oh, Jack, I'm so glad to see you but I'm scared for you, you shouldn't be here, they don't want me, they never did, they want you, or at least Victor wants you.'

'Who is this Victor?' Jack asked. 'The Bangers mentioned a Vic a few times on the way here.'

'He's their leader,' Katherine explained. 'Victor Bang is his name, hence why they are called the Bangers. He's rich and powerful and he's scoured the land for the meanest and stupidest morphers to do his dirty work. They get him what he wants and he pays them well for it. And for some reason, Jack, he wants you. I heard them discussing it several times. He seems to be obsessed with you. The Bangers don't know why, but he has been very insistent that they get you here. At first he told the Bangers to get your interrupter, that's when they attacked you in the alley. Since then though he's insisted he meet you in person. I don't know why he wants you, but, oh Jack, it can't be good. From what I hear, nothing Victor Bang ever does is good.'

She started sobbing again and Jack pulled her close against him. What could this Victor Bang possibly want with him? He did not have much; okay, he had some money left to him by his granddad, but from what Katherine had just said and the look of this house, Victor did not need money. He had his interrupter, which Victor Bang had obviously been interested in once, but he would not need Jack here in person for that. What else could there be? Jack could not think, in the back of his mind though a small voice said that he was bound to find out, sooner or later.

Once Katherine had calmed down enough to stop crying, Jack led her over to the enormous bed where they both sat down.

'So, tell me what happened after they took you,' Jack insisted, 'I was so worried about you, I had no idea where they had taken you or what they were going to do with you.'

'They brought me here,' Katherine said simply. 'They bundled me into the back of an old van and brought me here to this house, to this bedroom. I was so scared Jack. They've been keeping a very close eye on me; I thought I might be able to morph into Poppy and escape, so I tried. When they finally left me alone I managed to get the window open, I morphed and then I climbed out and jumped onto the path outside.'

She waved her hand vaguely in the direction of the window.

'It was quite high and I landed badly, jarring all my legs slightly, but I didn't even think about it, I just started running across the lawn towards some trees. I would have made it too, but I heard someone shout and looked behind me, which slowed me down a bit, and then something came racing after me. Jack, I'm fast as a cat but one of them can morph into a fox and he's even faster and he caught me, and… look.'

She held up her left leg and pulled the leg of her jeans up to reveal a large, bloody cut on her ankle.

'His teeth are very sharp, he dragged me back to the house by this leg.'

She pushed her jeans back into place. Jack remembered the small animal brushing past him in the alley the night before; a fox, yes of course that was what it had been. He felt anger at the sight of her injury and hugged her again.

She looked at him.

'How did you find me? How did they get you?' she asked.

Jack explained about the anonymous text he had received, 'So I went to the alley. It was the only place I could think of that they might be, and they were.'

'You got yourself caught on purpose?' she asked, astonished.

'Of course, I couldn't have found you otherwise. How would I know where to look?'

She stared at the floor. 'Oh, Jack, you shouldn't have come to rescue me, that's what they wanted, they took me so you would come to find me,' she said quietly.

Jack was quiet for a moment and then he said, 'But that really doesn't make any sense, I mean, I was there that day when they took you, I was with you, if they'd wanted me, why didn't they just take me?'

Katherine looked at him slightly puzzled.

'Er, I don't know,' she admitted. 'You're right though, why take me if it was you they wanted?'

Jack shrugged. 'Dunno, maybe they really are stupid,' he suggested.

They sat on the bed hugging each other for a while, both relieved to be with the other. After a while Jack got up and started pacing the room. He looked out the window; he could see the pathway that Katherine must have jumped to and the small clump of trees she must have been heading for. The grounds were quite vast, but around the house they were very open and they would be easily spotted if they tried to run. The window itself was old, presumably part of the original house: a large wooden frame with small glass panes with wooden bars separating them, typical Georgian in style. Although the window had locks that had obviously been fitted very recently, they were shiny brass. Jack knew enough to know that the glass was probably quite easy to break, (unlike new windows fitted with safety glass), so, although the noise would draw attention, it was an option, and it was likely that most of the windows in this house would be the same. He turned away from the window to look more closely at the rest of their prison. The large bed stood against one wall with the window on the right. Opposite the bed was an old fashioned dressing table with a mottled mirror and a stool whose cushion had seen better days. There was nothing else in the room apart from an oriental-looking rug at the end of the bed. There was another door next to the door Jack had come in through; Jack tried the handle and the door opened. He looked inside, it was dark. He moved further inside and found a light switch, he turned it on, the small room flooded with light; it was a bathroom. It was small and had no window, but it did have a bath, a toilet and a hand basin, they all looked old but clean. He came back out closing the door, there was certainly no way out there. Jack knew the main door was locked because he had heard it click earlier, but he tried the handle anyway. It moved downwards, but the door would not budge. He turned back to Katherine.

'Any ideas?' he asked.

She looked up at him, 'About what?' she asked in reply.

'On how to escape,' he said, as though it was obvious.

'Escape? We can't escape, weren't you listening? I've already tried.' she cried, 'There's no way out. They fitted those locks on the windows after my failed attempt. I can't move any of them now.'

Jack looked around the room again. 'There must be a way out. I didn't let the Bangers catch me just so I could sit here and let this Victor do what he wants with me,' he replied.

'But, Jack,' Katherine started.

'No, Kat,' Jack interrupted, 'we are not sitting here waiting for Victor or the Bangers to come back.'

Just as he said this, the lock turned on the door and the man called Rocket came in with a tray. He said nothing as he laid the tray just inside the door and then turned and left the room, locking the door again behind him. Jack looked at the tray; it had a large plate of sandwiches and a jug of what looked like orange squash. Jack felt his stomach rumble.

'Hungry?' he asked Katherine.

She nodded, they both sat on the floor and ate and drank in silence for a while.

Eventually Jack asked.

'What's this Victor like?'

She swallowed a bite of sandwich. 'I don't know, I've never seen him. Uncle Leo mentioned him a couple of times, I think they used to know each other or something.'

Katherine continued, 'Uncle Leo didn't like him though,

from what he said. He said he was evil, he said he would do anything to get what he wanted, he said what he wanted most of all was an interrupter, but the ones the Bangers kept getting for him weren't compatible or something. Uncle Leo said Victor Bang had offered him a small fortune to make one for him, but he refused. It sounded as though Victor got pretty upset and threatened Uncle Leo, and me, from what I can gather, but Uncle Leo would not be intimidated, he only gives discs to those who will not use them for wrong-doing.'

She moved position on the floor and took another bite of food. When she had swallowed it, she added, 'It must be your disc he wants, Jack. What else could it be?'

'Dunno,' Jack replied.

'But,' she added, 'why your disc? Why would he think your disc would work for him, when so many others haven't?'

Jack looked at her and shrugged, he wished he knew.

'I've been thinking,' Jack said thoughtfully. 'If this house belongs to Victor Bang, why do you think it's called Jackson Hall?'

Katherine looked at him. 'Hmm, I don't know, never really thought about it.'

The rest of the day passed slowly, they did not get any more visitors and eventually the light started to fade as night set in. Jack and Katherine sat huddled together on the large bed listening to the faint sounds in the house, none of which they could make out clearly. Although they had both heard shouting earlier, they had not been able to make out what was being said.

Jack awoke with a start, it still looked dark behind the curtains and it took him a few seconds to remember where he was. He looked at Katherine asleep beside him and smiled; she looked so beautiful, all the worry gone from her pretty face while she slept, though he guessed it would soon return once she woke up – their situation was not looking any better. He carefully removed her arm from around his waist and silently got up from the bed. He walked round the room, stretching his legs. He went over to the window and looked out, it was just starting to get light and the grounds looked deserted. He went into the tiny bathroom and splashed his face with cold water. He caught site of his face in the mirror. *What are you going to do, Jack?* he asked himself. He wished for the umpteenth time that he could morph quickly. What good would he be if they got the chance to run but he needed ten minutes to become the tailless dog? Katherine would have to go without him, that was the only possible option. She would be against it, of course, but he would make her; it was him they wanted after all. He heard the sound of movement from the bedroom and went back in, Katherine was sitting up, bleary eyed. She smiled when she saw him.

'Hi,' she said.

'Hi,' he replied, walking over to the bed and sitting down. 'You okay?'

'Yeah, s'pose,' she said, smiling weakly. 'You?'

'Yeah, course.' He kissed her on the cheek.

The rest of the day passed uneventfully, at about midday, or so it seemed by the angle of the sun, Jack could not be sure as neither of them had watches, the door was unlocked and a tray pushed into the room with sandwiches and squash, the same as the day before. Apart from that, they were left completely alone. They chatted, they stared out the window, they came up with elaborate plans for escaping, each one more ridiculous than the last and none of which would actually work.

'You're a polyskin, Jack, you could morph into an insect and crawl through the keyhole or you could morph into a bird and fly out the window or...' Katherine's ideas became wilder and wilder. Jack listened with a smile on his face.

'Great plan,' he would say every so often as she became

more and more carried away, 'But you seem to be forgetting about you in all these scenarios. Are you suggesting I carry you away on my back? Plus you also seem to be forgetting that morphing takes me a long time and I've never tried to become anything but a dog with no tail, and even that takes me far too long. And,' he added, 'the first time I tried to walk with four legs I fell over. Imagine me trying to fly!'

'Spoil-sport,' she teased.

On their third day in captivity, just as Jack was starting to get desperate thinking they would be stuck in this room forever, the lunch tray was delivered as usual but, as the door closed behind it, Jack did not hear the usual click of the lock. He waited for a few minutes to make sure whoever had been outside had time to disappear and then he got up and went over to the door. Feeling sure he was wrong and it would be locked, he tried the handle and both heard and felt the door open. Katherine looked up from where she was sitting on the floor, a sandwich halfway to her mouth. She stared in disbelief at the open door.

'Come on,' Jack whispered to her, 'this is our chance.' And he silently slipped out the door, Katherine a step behind him.

The problem with spur of the moment plans is there is no time to discuss them; sneaking along the landing, Jack had no idea where they were headed or what they would do when they got there. He also did not dare speak to Katherine, knowing what sensitive hearing morphers have he could not risk anyone hearing them. Jack was cross with himself for being unable to remember which way the stairs were from the bedroom they had been in, he had not taken any notice on the day they brought him in and was now wondering how he could be so careless. He chanced a glance behind him at Katherine; she was crouched low, carefully treading as quietly as possible with a terrified look on her face. He looked forward again and

his heart leaped as he saw the top of the curving staircase, he
had come the right way after all, but just as he was starting
to relax slightly at the thought that they could soon be free,
he heard someone speaking. Craning his neck he caught sight
of the top of someone's head coming up the stairs. Panicking,
he turned to Katherine who had also heard the talking, and
motioned with his hand for her to turn around and go the
other way. She did not need telling twice. They both took off
at double speed in the direction they had just come. Neither of
them could remember which door they had come out, there
were so many doors on the landing and they all looked the
same. Jack was very reluctant to go back into the same room,
but at least they knew what was in there. Choosing the nearest
one, Jack tried the handle and the door opened, they both
hurried inside. It was not the room they had come from; it
was a bedroom, but it was quite different from the one they
had been imprisoned in. It was about the same size, but it was
a lot more modern in the way it was furnished and decorated
and Jack got the feeling this room was probably used a lot
more frequently. He quickly closed the door behind him and
pressed his ear to it to hear the man coming up the stairs.
He could not hear anything. Assuming the man had turned
the other way at the top of the stairs, Jack opened the door a
crack and saw someone disappearing down the corridor in the
opposite direction.

Breathing a sigh of relief, he turned to Katherine. 'It's okay,
he's gone the other way, come on.'

Taking Katherine's hand he pulled her from the room and
back onto the landing. After a quick check up and down to
make sure the coast was clear, Jack dragged Katherine towards
the stairs and they both ran down them as quickly and quietly
as possible. Once at the bottom, they hurried across the vast
hall towards the front door. Jack could not believe their luck
– they had not bumped into anyone. He grabbed the door

handle and a sinking feeling told him their luck had just run out. Coming up the outside steps towards them were three men, two of them were Bangers Jack had seen before, but the man in front Jack had never seen before; he was tall and thin with a thin face. He wore aviator sunglasses, even though it was not sunny, and was dressed in an old-fashioned, black velvet tailcoat and britches, a white shirt that had ruffles down the front and at the cuffs and a top hat, giving him the look of a nineteenth century lord of the manor. He saw Jack standing on the other side of the door through the glass window and smiled. He opened the door from the outside and walked through, still smiling. He removed his hat and Jack could see he had long dark hair that was pulled back into a ponytail and was slightly receding at the temples. He also removed his sunglasses to reveal black eyes.

'Well, Jack, we meet at last,' he said in a pleasant voice as he held out his hand, looking like he wanted to shake Jack's hand.

'I'm Victor,' he said.

As he said this, he curled his thumb upwards and his two smallest fingers into his fist, pointing the other two fingers at Jack so his hand resembled a gun.

'Bang,' he added.

14.

The Telling Cups

Jack pushed Katherine behind him so he was shielding her with his body and started backing away from Victor and the Bangers.

Victor smiled. 'Don't look so worried, Jack, my hand is not loaded.'

He laughed heartily at his own joke.

Jack's heart was pounding in his chest and, much to his annoyance, he could feel the prickling sensation all over him that told him fur was growing. A growl started deep within him and ripped loudly from his body, surprising even him with its ferocity.

'Now, now, Jack,' Victor said soothingly, holding his hand out palm down and waving it gently. 'Calm down, I don't want to hurt you.'

'Yeah right,' Jack snarled. 'What do you want with us then?'

'I want to talk to you, get to know you, show you around my beautiful home,' Victor replied, waving his left arm around the hall. 'I'll admit you have something I want, Jack, but if you cooperate there is no reason for anyone to get hurt, I mean that.'

Victor took a tentative step towards Jack, who instinctively took another step backwards, pushing Katherine with him.

'You want me to get 'im, boss?' one of the Bangers asked, pushing his shirtsleeves up above his elbows.

'No, Filbert, Jack will be fine when he calms down,' Victor said to the man, then, turning back to Jack, 'are you calming down, Jack?'

Jack felt anything but calm, but he knew he needed to control the morphing that had started; the last thing he needed was to lose control and give Victor even more of an advantage.

'I'm fine, don't worry about me,' Jack said through gritted teeth, never taking his eyes from Victor.

'Oh, I'm not worried, Jack. I never worry about anything; I would like to get on though. I'm a busy man,' he paused, then added, 'So would you like to see around my house?'

Jack was puzzled; he knew there was no way Victor just wanted to show him around, there was obviously something or somewhere he had in mind. However ominous this situation seemed, Jack could not help thinking a tour of this enormous house might buy him time to think and possibly present another chance for escape. He looked Victor straight in the eye.

'Okay,' he said.

He heard Katherine let out a little squeak behind him and he squeezed her hand in what he hoped was a reassuring way.

'Splendid,' said Victor, sounding genuinely pleased. 'Let's start over here,' and he pointed to large double doors on his left. Jack walked half sideways towards the double doors, keeping Victor in his peripheral vision and holding tightly to Katherine's hand. They entered the room; it was very large with ceiling to floor glass doors at the far end, which looked like they opened onto a large garden patio. The room was comfortably furnished as a living room with two squashy settees facing a huge flat-screen television. Occasional tables and small chests of drawers lined the walls, holding china figurines and vases of flowers.

'I love this room,' Victor said, almost to himself. 'When the sun shines it's so light and warm.'

He looked at Jack expectantly, 'Well, what do you think?'

'S'okay,' Jack said suspiciously, he really did not care what the room was like.

'Splendid,' said Victor. 'Let's move on.' And he marched back out the double doors into the hall.

The same thing happened with several more rooms; they visited three more living rooms, two dining rooms, a huge modern kitchen, more bedrooms than Jack could remember, no less than five bathrooms and even the garage, which was attached to the house and accessible from a small door in the hall. Finally they came to the biggest doors of all, huge double doors at least twice the width of a normal door and so tall they almost reached the very high ceiling. Jack could sense the excitement in Victor. *This is it*, he thought, *this is what this charade has been all about. This is the room Victor wants me to see.* Victor took an enormous key from the inside of his jacket and made a show of putting it in the lock and turning it. The doors creaked as they were pushed open to reveal what Jack could only assume used to be a ballroom. It was huge: great arched windows lined the walls showing a beautiful patio area outside on the left and massive crystal chandeliers hung from the elaborately decorated ceiling which was at least two floors high. The floor was polished wood that gleamed dully in the faint light. What surprised Jack most about this room was that there was no furniture in it, no chairs, no tables not even a rug. The only thing in the room was right in the middle; placed directly on the floor was a polished metal rack, in grooves on the metal rack were six metal cups of varying sizes. Jack looked at Victor, he was smiling the smug smile of someone who knew the answer to the question on everyone's lips and was just dying for someone to ask it. Victor looked at Jack, his smile got wider.

'Well, Jack, what do you think?' he asked, slightly breathless.

'About what?' Jack asked.

Victor's smiled faltered. 'Do you need a closer look? Come,' he ordered and he started towards the centre of the room. Everyone followed him. Now he was closer, Jack could see the cups in more detail. The largest cup was the size of a bucket; the smallest was the size of a small teacup. They were all silver in colour and engraved with moons and stars and inlaid with precious-looking stones in a rainbow of colours. Jack felt a strange feeling looking at the cups, but he did not know why. He looked at Victor.

'Do you know what these are, Jack?' Victor asked.

'No,' said Jack honestly.

'These are the Telling Cups,' Victor said dramatically and Jack half expected an orchestra to start playing.

He heard Katherine draw in a sharp breath. He looked at her quizzically, but she shook her head. He turned back to look at Victor.

'And what are the Telling Cups?' Jack asked.

Victor smiled.

'The Telling Cups are very old and very valuable,' Victor started. 'No one knows exactly how old or where they came from originally, but they have magical powers. They have another name, a proper name, their real name. The seven something's, er, chalices of something, I don't know, doesn't matter really. It is said that when all the Telling Cups are together and filled with certain, well somethings, they will reveal the answers to all your questions. They know everything...' he trailed off dramatically, looking at Jack.

Victor walked slowly around the metal rack, staring lovingly at the cups. When he got back round to where Jack was standing, he asked, 'Do you see I have a problem, Jack?'

And he pointed to the very end of the rack next to the smallest cup. Jack looked where he was pointing and saw an extra groove at the end, smaller than all the others, he looked back at Victor and Victor smiled.

'I see you can see my problem, Jack,' Victor said. 'Alas, the Telling Cups are not complete; there is one missing, the smallest one, and without it they will not work at all.' He paused and then added, 'I have searched and searched, but so far have had no luck. So that's what I need you for, do you know where that missing cup is, Jack?'

Jack looked stunned, why should he know where it was?

'No,' he said.

Victor looked at him, his expression harder and colder than before.

'Think, Jack, think. A throwaway comment, something left lying around, didn't Charles ever mention the missing cup? I know he had it,' Victor said.

'Who's Charles?' asked Jack.

'*Who's Charles?*' Victor mimicked. 'Don't play games with me, Jack.'

'I'm not playing games, I don't know anyone called Charles,' Jack said honestly. 'And I'd never even heard of the Telling Cups until you just told me.'

Now it was Victor's turn to look stunned.

'Surely you jest, Jack?' he asked.

Seeing the blank look on Jack's face, Victor started to laugh.

'Can this be? Can this really be true? You don't know who Charles is? Well, Jack, I must say I had not expected this.' Victor looked away, deep in thought and then he said something under his breath that Jack could not hear. He turned back to Jack.

'It would appear that it is up to me to enlighten you into our family history, Jack.' He paused and Jack said, '*Our* family history?'

Victor smiled.

'Yes, *our* family history. You see, Jack, Charles was my brother, my older brother,' he said.

'Was?' asked Jack quietly.

'Yes, I'm afraid my poor dear brother has departed this

world, although his heart lives on,' he pointed at Jack's chest and smiled knowingly raising his eyebrows.

Jack put his hand over his own chest and Victor nodded.

'You mean... are you saying...that... I mean,' Jack's heart was pounding and his breath was coming very fast. 'Um, is it true... my heart?' he looked at Victor.

'How eloquent,' said Victor, 'I couldn't have put it better myself. Yes, Jack, my brother's heart beats in your chest. I must say, I thought that awful Dr Noah would have told you.'

Jack felt Katherine tense at the mention of her uncle.

Jack felt faint; Victor Bang had a brother and it had been his heart that had been given to Jack during his operation, this was a lot to take in. He had often wondered about the man who had been knocked over by that lorry, but in Jack's mind he had always been faceless, nameless, just *a man*. Now, suddenly, he was a real person, with a name and a family. Jack took some deep breaths.

'I'm sorry,' Jack said to Victor, 'I didn't know.'

Victor laughed.

'Don't be, we were not exactly close. Of course, he would have been delighted to give his heart to you, he would have been so proud,' Victor continued.

Jack didn't understand this.

'Why?' he asked.

Victor stared at Jack for a few moments, then he said, 'Jack, I said this was *our* family history; Charles was not only my brother, he was your father.'

The words hung in the air, for a few seconds they made no sense to Jack at all.

'He was what?' he asked eventually.

'Jack, please try to keep up,' Victor said impatiently. 'He was your father, your dad, your papa, whatever you want to call him.'

Jack slumped to the floor, still holding Katherine's hand and pulling her with him. He was almost gasping for air. His father? The man he had never known? The man whose name he had never even known?

'My father?' he asked quietly, looking up at Victor.

'Yes,' Victor replied simply.

'I have my father's heart?'

'How many times am I going to have to repeat myself, Jack? Yes, yes, yes, my brother, your father, his heart – all clear?' Victor almost shouted.

'Charles Bang was my father?' Jack said almost to himself.

'What? No, not Charles Bang. Bang is my name, well, a name I gave myself. Whenever someone asked my name I would always say, Victor and then pretend to shoot them with my hand and say, Bang, just like I did with you and it sort of stuck.' Victor looked proudly at Jack, expecting him to be impressed or at least find his story amusing. When he saw Jack's blank expression he continued, 'Charles Jackson was your father, where do you think your name came from, or the name of this house for that matter? This was your father's house Jack,' Victor explained. 'But when he, well, fell, or whatever, it became mine.'

'What do mean, or whatever?' asked Jack, with a feeling of dread creeping over him.

Victor looked unsure what to say next, then, seemingly making his mind up, he said, 'Okay, it won't hurt to tell you because, well, you won't be telling anyone will you.'

Jack thought this was more of a statement than a question.

'Okay, Charles and I never really got on, even as kids. He was the clever one, he was my parents – your grandparents – favourite. Charles Jackson was everyone's favourite. But he wasn't as great as everyone thought, you know, wasn't as honest as he made out. You see I knew him better than anyone. When he left school he went travelling for a couple of years; he never told anyone where he was going and when he came back he never told anyone where he had been, but he came back a very rich man, a very rich man indeed. He bought this house and moved my parents and me in. He always resented me being here, but I wasn't about to give up the high life, not after I'd had a taste of it. He refused to say where and how he had got the money, but I suspected it was not all above board, if you know what I mean? He kept a lot of secrets and I mean a lot of secrets. He always kept this room locked, always. No one was allowed in here except him, not even to clean it and he used to spend hours locked in here. No one even knew what was in here, not even my parents, though they didn't care, they were so proud of Charles because he'd made something of himself. In case I haven't mentioned this, by the way, I'm a polyskin, just as I assume you are and my dear brother was. Anyway, I spent a lot of time devising a plan. One day, when he was out, I morphed into a mouse. Something that small is very painful to become, but it was worth it. I flattened my tiny body so it would fit under the crack at the bottom of these doors and forced my way into this room. I found these cups, Jack. I had no idea what they were, but I knew they were something to do with Charles' fortune. I have never seen all seven together, Jack, Charles, I found out, never left the house without the smallest cup with him. I began to research the cups; this was not easy, they are not well known. Charles had found them and discovered how to use them to get the answers to all his questions. I eventually found someone who had heard of them and their magical powers and he told me what he knew, which was not much, but enough to make me realise I was right. I wanted these cups, Jack, wanted them very badly. I bided my time, no need to rush into these things. Once both my parents had died, I knew if I could only get rid of Charles, this house, the money and the cups would be mine. Then I found out about you, that was an unexpected blow, I admit, but nothing I can't handle,' he winked at Jack. 'It took me years, Jack, years to get the right opportunity but one day it came, quite out of the blue. I used to follow Charles everywhere, waiting for a chance to steal the cup. If I'm honest, I never intended to kill him, just take everything he owned, but when the chance came it was too good to turn down.' Victor paused, as if remembering some sweet memory. He sighed and then continued, 'I saw him standing at the side of the road, a lorry was thundering down the road. Without thinking, I morphed into a cat and tangled myself around his legs. He lost his balance and well, the rest you know. There was an awful kerfuffle; lots of people screaming and running, so much going on that nobody noticed the small cat slipping away. I got the house, the money and the cups and you got a heart, everyone's a winner.' Victor finished dramatically sweeping his arms around as if to point to all he owned.

'Except my dad. He didn't win,' Jack said in horror. 'You killed your own brother.'

'Well, almost everyone,' corrected Victor in an off-hand manner. 'I didn't get the smallest cup though, Jack, in all the mayhem caused by the '*accident*'.' On the word accident, Victor used the index and middle fingers of each hand to make inverted commas in the air. 'I didn't get the chance to search Charles' pockets; too many people around, I couldn't morph. I know he had it on him, though, so what happened to it?'

Victor looked annoyed.

'So, you really don't know anything about the missing cup, then?' he said, but more to himself than Jack. Jack shook his head.

'Damn,' Victor swore. He paced up and down, apparently in thought. 'Okay,' he said after a while, 'all is not lost. So you can't help me with the cup, I can see that, but you can still help me in my other quest, there's no doubt about that.'

He turned his face to Jack and Jack saw that his expression was now greedy and mean.

'You still have something I want,' and he looked at Jack's left arm.

Jack instinctively covered his disc with his right hand.

'Yes, that's right, Jack, I want that disc. As we are blood family it is more likely it will be a compatible match with my blood and tissue type. After all, Charles' heart was a match for you, wasn't it?' He smiled, but it was cold and heartless and Jack felt shivers up and down his spine.

'I'm not an unreasonable man, Jack. I don't want to hurt you. If you cooperate I have a very good surgeon standing by to remove it painlessly.' He looked at the two Bangers standing behind Jack, who was still sitting on the floor clutching Katherine.

'On the other hand,' Victor continued, 'if you don't cooperate, I'm sure one of my friends here can remove it the quick way.'

The Bangers laughed.

'And why should I give you my disc?' Jack asked, sounding a lot braver than he felt.

Victor knelt down beside him and grabbed Katherine by the wrist, staring right into Jack's eyes, he spoke, and this time his voice was cold and hard without any trace of pretend friendliness. 'Because if you don't,' he said, his eyes not leaving Jack's, 'I'll kill your little girlfriend.'

15.

Victor's Victory

A long tube was trailing along the floor; one end was attached to a machine and the other end to a needle that was inserted under Jack's skin on his left hand. Jack lay nervously on a bed in one of the many bedrooms in Jackson Hall. It was not the same bedroom he and Katherine had shared when they had first arrived, this bedroom had been furnished to look like a hospital room. Two surgical-looking beds sat side by side along the furthest wall from the door. Lots of impressive state-of-the-art-looking equipment bleeped and hissed as lights flashed on and off and things rose and fell in a rhythmic chant. The surgeon, that Victor had previously referred to, was a weedy-looking man who wore green scrubs and plastic clogs, but Jack suspected these were as near to any medical training as he had ever had. He fussed around checking machines, trying to look like he knew what he was doing, but Jack thought he looked nervous and scared and he kept glancing at Victor as if seeking approval. Victor was on the other bed, a long tube attached to a machine trailing from his arm as well. Victor did not look nervous or scared; on the contrary, Victor was looking very pleased with himself, evidently this was something Victor was looking forward to. He looked over and smiled at Jack.

'Come now, nephew, it's not so bad. Just a few more minutes and it'll all be over. I'll have your disc and you, well, you won't need it anymore.'

This was the second time Victor had referred to Jack's immediate future, or lack of it, and Jack's feeling of foreboding was increasing. Katherine was not in the room, Jack had not seen her since they had parted in the hall for him and Victor to come upstairs to this room and two of the Bangers had led her off to one of the rooms off the hall; Jack could not remember what the room was and wished he had paid more attention on the so-called tour. The surgeon, who since Jack had been in the room had only been referred to as Doc, adjusted his very thick glasses and stared at one of the bleeping machines.

'Are we anywhere near ready?' Victor asked impatiently.

Doc glanced nervously at Victor and away again quickly.

'Yes, nearly, nearly ready,' he mumbled, shuffling to the next machine.

After about another twenty minutes of Doc shuffling from machine to machine and Victor tutting loudly, Doc suddenly announced he was ready.

'Okay,' he said, walking towards Jack with a very sharp looking scalpel. 'Let's get this show on the road.'

Jack could see the scalpel cutting into the taut flesh on the inside of his wrist, but could not feel any pain; he was sufficiently numb from whatever Doc was pumping into his system. He watched as Doc carefully used the knife to make an incision about two inches long and then peeled the skin away from the disc. He could see his blood pumping in his veins and he had to give Doc his dues, he was being very careful, he had not cut any veins or arteries, which Jack was very grateful for. Doc carefully prised the disc from its resting place, removing any surplus growths that had connected to it and cutting the main fleshy stem that attached it to Jack with a swift and final cut. So the disc that had caused Jack so much interest and discomfort was no longer part of him, it sat in Doc's palm, vibrating slightly. It was silvery in colour, the size and shape of a two-pound coin; it had small bumps all over the surface and small hole right in the middle. Jack looked away from the disc to Victor, who was staring greedily, almost licking his lips, at the disc. Victor had clearly waited a long time for this moment. Doc put the disc carefully into a surgical tray full of some sort of clear liquid and started stitching Jack's skin together; again he felt no pain, but physical pain was not the thing he was most worried about right now. Stitching complete, Doc bandaged Jack's wrist.

'There,' he announced. 'All done.'

Doc turned to Victor, smiling.

'Your turn,' he said triumphantly.

Jack sat on his bed, watching Doc get to work on Victor; he made a similar incision in Victor's wrist and peeled the skin back. He placed a long silver instrument, which looked like a large toothpick with a hook on the end, into the wound and carefully felt around inside with it; when he had located what he was looking for he pulled slightly and a fleshy stem popped out of Victor's wrist, similar to the one Doc had cut in Jack's wrist that had set the disc free. Carefully picking up the disc he shook it to remove the excess liquid and then placed it over the cut, pushing it under the skin and into place with the toothpick thing. Once he was happy with the position, he used the toothpick thing to lift the fleshy stem and place it over the disc and then he and Victor watched and waited. At first Jack could not see anything, it seemed to him they were staring at nothing, but then slowly he saw the fleshy stem start to move very slightly. It wriggled and stretched and snaked its way slowly over the bumpy surface of the disc, it moved backwards and forwards several times until it finally stopped and then, with a small sucking noise, it latched into the hole in the centre of the disc. The disc started vibrating even harder until it was making a buzzing noise. Jack watched in macabre fascination as the disc physically jumped a couple of times, still buzzing and vibrating quite strongly before it fell back into place, vibrating lightly as it had before. Victor looked at Doc, a look of questioning expectation on his face. Doc smiled in response.

'Looks good,' he breathed. 'Looks really good.'

Victor smiled triumphantly and made a sound that was a sort of cross between a happy whoop and a relieved sigh. Doc started stitching Victor's wound and when he was finished he bandaged Victor's wrist, just as he had with Jack. Doc fussed around a bit more, removing the needles from the backs of Jack and Victor's hands and spraying what smelled like alcohol over all the machines and surfaces. Victor got up from his bed; he stretched, looked at his bandaged wrist, touched it lightly and then smiled. He looked at Jack.

'That wasn't so hard, was it? Not even any pain.'

'Where's Katherine?' Jack asked, not caring about anything else.

Victor stared at Jack for a few seconds and then he smiled again.

'Good question,' he said slowly. 'Yes, she should be here by now,' he looked at Doc. 'See what's keeping them, will you?' he demanded.

Doc shuffled out of the room.

A few minutes later Doc re-entered the room, followed by Katherine and two of the Bangers. Jack was relieved to see that, although she looked scared, Katherine did not appear to be harmed in any way. Jack smiled at her and she gave him a small, watery smile in response. One of the Bangers, Kev, the short fat one, pushed Katherine in the back, making her move more quickly towards the bed Jack had just vacated. Jack realised with alarm that Katherine was expected to climb onto the bed.

'What's going on?' he asked, his voice sounding slightly hysterical. 'What are you doing to Katherine?'

'For goodness sake, Jack,' Victor moaned. 'You're not very bright are you? I know I have my own disc now.' He lightly touched his bandaged wrist and nodded his head to Jack in mock thanks. 'But my Bangers still need discs and, as she's here, well, you never know, we might get lucky.'

Jack could feel his anger rising; he could again feel the familiar prickling of growing fur all over his body and the breathless, heart thumping adrenalin that warned him the morphing process was starting. *Calm down,* he told himself, *a ten minute morph into the tailless dog will not help anyone right now, least of all Katherine.*

'No,' he gasped. 'Leave her alone, I'll… I'll… I'll—'

Victor looked at him almost laughing.

'You'll what? You'll… you'll… you'll w-w-w-what?'

Victor laughed at his own joke.

'Leave her alone,' Jack repeated, and then, in a small voice, he added, 'Please.'

Victor looked at him.

'Touching,' he remarked without conviction.

A noise in the hall outside caught everyone's attention, as they all looked towards the door, it opened and a tall, slim, elegant woman walked in. She had wavy, waist-length hair that was dyed blonde with at least an inch of dark re-growth. She had olive skin and she wore a tight, pale pink suit with a very short skirt and large sunglasses. When Victor saw her, his face broke into a genuine smile.

'Demetria, darling,' he exclaimed with obvious affection. 'Your timing is perfect.' He held up his bandaged wrist.

Demetria put her hand up to her sunglasses and pulled them down to the end of her nose so she could peer over the top.

'*Veectorr*,' she said in a heavily accented voice, rolling the letter 'r' at the end of Victor's name. 'Where you were? Why you no came? I wait, but you don't came.' She finished her sentence with an exaggerated pout.

'But, darling,' Victor cooed, holding his arms out and embracing her. 'I sent word with Alfie; he was supposed to let you know that my plans had, well, changed.'

Victor shot a menacing look over Demetria's shoulder at the tall Banger with the bald head and scar who blushed and looked slightly alarmed.

'I'll deal with you later,' Victor hissed at Alfie, who swallowed hard.

His attention back on Demetria; he kissed her cheek and then pulled out of the embrace and held her with just his right arm.

'Look,' he said excitedly, holding up his bandaged wrist again. 'Look, I have it, I finally have it.'

She removed her sunglasses and stared at the bandage for a few seconds.

'I can see,' Demetria said, she looked at Jack.

'Is that 'im?' she asked. 'Is 'e Sharles' boy?'

Victor joined her in staring at Jack.

'Yes, that's Jack,' Victor confirmed.

''E no look like Sharles,' she commented and walked closer to Jack, staring at him.

Jack looked into her face, she was an attractive woman, but by no means pretty; her features were heavy, her nose too long and beak-like and her chin too square. She had certainly made the best of herself though; her clothes and make-up were immaculate and, as she drew closer, Jack was almost over-powered by the smell of expensive perfume. As she stared at Jack he started to feel uncomfortable. He looked into her eyes and noticed that one of her eyes was dark brown but the other one was half dark brown and half green. Jack felt a slight jolt in his stomach, he was sure he had seen those eyes somewhere before, but before he had time to think too much about it, she seemed to grow bored of looking at him and looked back at Victor.

'You 'aff the leetle cup?' she asked, one eyebrow raised.

'Ah, no, not exactly,' replied Victor, looking slightly uncomfortable. 'It appears Jack and Charles weren't exactly close. Going to have to rethink that one, I'm afraid.'

She seemed to lose interest at these words.

'When we go?' she asked, looking down at her expertly manicured nails.

'Er, soon, darling,' Victor assured her. 'I just need to finish a few things here and then we can go.'

'But I bored, Veectorr,' she whined, running a playful fingernail lightly down his cheek and licking her lips.

Victor swallowed.

'Darling,' he said. 'How about I get Kev to drive you now and I'll meet you there?' As he said this, he pulled a fat wad of money out of his pocket and, peeling off several notes, he pressed them into her eagerly awaiting hand. She smiled, exposing expensive white teeth and blew him a kiss as she stuffed the money into her already open and waiting handbag. Then she turned on her heel and walked towards the door, Kev running to keep up with her long strides.

'See you layter, Veectorr, babee,' she said without looking back at him and she left the room. The door closed behind her and Victor's attention turned back to Doc and Katherine.

'Well, what are you waiting for?' he snapped. 'We haven't got all day.'

Doc jumped and immediately hustled Katherine onto the recently vacated bed and started pushing a long needle none too carefully into the back of her hand. Jack saw Katherine wince as the needle went into her vein and his anger rose again, causing a snarl deep in his throat. The noise made Doc and Victor both turn to look at him, Doc immediately turned back to Katherine and the job in hand; Victor stared at Jack for a few seconds before laughing.

'Really, Jack, you must learn to control that temper of yours, it'll get you into trouble one day.' He turned back to watch Doc, leaving Jack angrier than ever.

Jack watched as Doc repeated the same procedure on Katherine that he had performed on Jack just a short while earlier. He watched as the scalpel cut a long incision into Katherine's skin, he watched as the fleshy stem that connected the disc to Katherine was cut and the softly vibrating disc was removed and placed in a bowl of clear liquid. Doc looked expectantly at Victor, who immediately looked around the room, his eyes fell on the tall Banger, Alfie, who was looking slightly sheepish.

'Alfie, it's your lucky day,' Victor said and pointed at the vacant bed.

Alfie looked a mixture of scared and pleased as he slowly walked towards the empty bed. As he climbed up onto it, Doc shoved a needle deep into his hand and he let out a low hiss and shot Doc a look that said he had better be more careful. Doc flinched, but carried on. Once Alfie's wound was opened, Doc got the disc he had removed from Katherine and pushed it into place between the flesh. Doc used the toothpick thing to locate Alfie's fleshy stem. Once found, it coiled and snaked its way across the disc, just as Victor's had, but as it located the middle of the disc, instead of attaching itself as Victor's had, it rose up so it was standing upright out of the cut, it started shaking quite hard and after a few seconds blood started coming out of the end. Doc immediately grabbed the disc and wrenched it out of Alfie's arm. As he did this the fleshy stem stopped shaking and relaxed back down where it had come from. Doc turned to Victor.

'Sorry,' he said. 'Not a match; this disc will not work for Alfie.'

Victor looked momentarily disappointed but recovered quickly and said.

'Pity, but never mind. Wrap it up Doc, we'll try it on Kev later.'

Doc shuffled around packing the disc in some wet cotton wool and sealing it in a plastic bag. Then as if only just realising he had not sewn Katherine's arm back up he set about that. Jack caught Katherine's tearful gaze and wished there was something he could do. As soon as Katherine was finished with, she was pushed off the bed; she half stumbled, half ran to Jack's side and grabbed his hand, holding on to it as if her life depended on it.

'Alfie, take them back to their bedroom for a while. They'll need some rest,' Victor ordered. Then, looking at Jack, he added, 'especially him; he'll need all the strength he can get.' He smiled to himself and then left the room.

Back in the same bedroom they had stayed in before, Jack and Katherine sat on the bed holding each other very tightly. Katherine had her head on Jack's shoulder and was crying quietly.

'What do you think he's going to do with us?' she sobbed.

Jack pulled away from Katherine slightly and held her tear-stained face in his hands.

'I don't know,' he replied honestly, looking into her eyes. 'I think it's too much to hope that he'll just let us walk out of here. He promised he wouldn't hurt us,' he added without much conviction.

'I don't think Victor Bang will care much about breaking that promise, do you?' Katherine asked.

'Guess not,' Jack replied, pulling her close again.

The anaesthetic was beginning to wear off and Jack's left

arm was starting to throb painfully. Jack had never been very fond of his interrupter; it had bothered him ever since it had been fitted, itching, vibrating and looking weird, pulling his skin so tight. Now that it was gone, however, he missed it more than he could have imagined. He did not even want to think about what might happen if he was unable to control his temper and accidently morphed into the tailless dog. How long would it take for him to lose his mind? He knew he had the back-up disc, Dr Noah had provided them both with these extra discs, set deep in their right wrists, but just how effective were they? Did they do the same job or were they only a temporary measure? Why had he not thought to ask? *Because you never really believed anyone would take the other disc, did you?* A small voice in his head asked. *No,* he replied honestly to himself. Jack heard Katherine give a soft snore and realised she must have fallen asleep. Moving very carefully, he managed to lie down with Katherine at his side without disturbing her. *Best if we could both get some sleep,* he thought. After all hadn't Victor said they would need their strength? He closed his eyes.

It seemed like only seconds later that a noise outside the door woke Jack up. Looking around sleepily he realised it was dark outside; several hours must have passed. Katherine was stirring, so he moved out from under her arm and got rather unsteadily to his feet. A loud click told him the door to their room was being unlocked. He stood watching the door while it slowly opened. A man came in the room, he was quite non-descript, average height, average weight, short mousey hair and a very ordinary face. Jack could not remember ever seeing him before. He spoke in a very bland voice.

'Victor is waiting to see you,' he said without emotion.

Then he just stood there waiting. Katherine was now fully awake and standing next to Jack. They looked at each other and, deciding they had very little choice, moved towards the door and the bland man. As they moved, he turned and walked out the door and they followed. Walking down the long hallway it occurred to Jack to try to run for it, but, although the house seemed very quiet, his arm was now very painful and he was sure Katherine's must be too. Just how far did he think they would get? He abandoned the idea almost as soon as he had it. They reached the large double doors that told Jack they were going back into the room with the Telling Cups. The man in front of them pushed one door and it creaked open very slowly. The room was exactly as it had been earlier that day, but with one noticeable difference: there was now a chair in the middle of the room, placed at the end where the missing smallest cup should have been and, sitting on that chair, his legs crossed and his hands brought together under his chin as if in prayer, was Victor Bang. He smiled when he saw Jack and Katherine, but he did not move; he remained seated and still as they approached him.

As they drew near to him he said, 'Ah, Jack, I trust you got some sleep.' It was a statement rather than a question and he carried on without waiting for Jack to reply.

'I must say, I myself am feeling most refreshed, though I have not slept. I think your disc is giving me added energy and for that I thank you.' He gave Jack a little bow of his head. 'Regrettably, I have other things I must now attend to; my time is very precious you know. Before I go, however, there is one last thing I need both of you to do for me. As I mentioned before you won't be needing your discs because from now on,' he looked at Katherine, 'You will be living as that adorable little cat you're so fond of, and you,' he turned to Jack, 'Will be living as that monstrous dog you rather favour. After all, I can't have you running back to Dr Noah and telling him all the things you've learned here, can I? No, that would never do. I'd really rather not have to kill you both, that would be very messy and time consuming so to be avoided if at all possible. No, the best course of action is if you both voluntarily morph into your animal forms; without your discs you will not remember much for very long, my Bangers will wait until they are sure you cannot re-morph into human form and then they will let you go. You will be none the wiser, believing you have always been animals. Everyone's happy.' He finished, looking immensely proud of his plan.

So that was the plan, for Jack and Katherine to live as animals and never be able to tell anyone what had happened at Jackson Hall and the things Victor had told them about how he had killed Charles. No wonder he had been so open and honest.

'Well?' Victor had said a few minutes later when no one had moved. 'What are we waiting for? Why aren't you morphing?'

Jack took a quick look around the room; there was no escape. He looked at Katherine, she was looking at him, he smiled and she smiled weakly back at him. He looked at Victor who was looking a mixture of expectant and slightly bored. Jack took Katherine's hand and squeezed it. Then, hoping and praying that their back-up discs would last long enough, he felt the familiar prickling sensation all over his body that told him the morphing process was beginning.

16.

The Escape

They both stood before Victor as animals. Katherine was shivering slightly even though it was not cold. The little cat looked terrified. As usual it had taken Katherine only a couple of minutes to assume the shape of Poppy, Jack's transformation had been a lot slower. Jack's morphing into Prince the tailless dog had always been a long and painful process, but he had managed to get it down to under five minutes; this time, however, it took a lot longer and was a lot more painful. Whether this was down to the fact that he was being forced to morph when he did not want to, or whether his subconscious was holding him back because he knew his interrupter was missing and he did not have full trust in the back-up disc, he did not know, but whatever it was it took him nearly half an hour of excruciating pain to assume the dog form. Writhing and calling out, Jack had forced himself to endure the sort of pain he would have called a halt to under normal circumstances; it had been hard for Poppy to watch, she had buried her head between her paws and winced at every noise he made. The fur had grown first and the limbs had followed one by one, each slight change in shape and size causing flesh and bone and muscle to stretch and rip. When his left arm had morphed, the tight bandage covering the place the disc had been removed from, had fallen off and fresh blood had started to ooze from between the stitches. Jack's body had followed the limbs; his back had arched in agony as his spine had contracted, his ribcage had tightened and his waist had pulled inward. The tail had started to grow, but Jack had managed to halt the process before it got too far and so had been left with a stump about two inches long. Lastly his head had changed; already covered in fur Jack's nose had stretched and elongated into the dog's snout, his ears had also stretched and flopped over and his teeth had grown pointy and long to look like fangs.

Panting from the effort and pain he now stood watching Victor, who was still sitting in the chair, but by now was looking incredulous having witnessed Jack's transformation.

'Good Lord, Jack!' Victor exclaimed eventually, once he was sure Jack had actually finished changing.

'That was the worst bit of morphing I've ever seen! You're going to thank me for taking your disc, you'll never have to go through that awful process again.'

He laughed to himself but then looked serious, he stared at both the tailless dog and the little cat.

'Well, now, let's see. A couple of hours should do it,' he looked at Poppy.

'You should go first, my dear. After all it took nearly half an hour for your hopeless boyfriend to morph, so he'll have the pleasure of watching you, well, you know,' he smiled, turning to Prince.

'And you, finally, well you can watch kitty here and then you won't have long to wait until, well, you join her.'

Prince growled, teeth bared.

'Yes, yes, you're angry, I get it,' Victor said impatiently. 'But the good news is, you won't remember any of this soon.'

He got up and started pacing around the Telling Cups. The

room was silent except for the sound of Victor's shoes on the floor. After three laps of the cups, Victor stopped, he stared at the little cat and the tailless dog for a few seconds and then announced, 'Well, with all the excitement I almost forgot that I have my own adventure to start. I've been so busy thinking about you two and the lives you will lead from now on that I haven't given any thought to my new life.'

As soon as he finished speaking, he himself started to morph. As with everyone else he was much quicker than Jack and on a par with Katherine, so a couple of minutes later he stood in front of them as a cat. Not a cat like Poppy, who was small and pretty, this cat was black and huge, more the size of a dog with features that were more akin to lions or tigers than domestic cats; it looked like no real cat Jack had ever seen and he assumed it was a product of Victor's imagination. It stared at Prince with Victor's black eyes, not blinking. Jack felt uncomfortable under the big cat's stare and looked away towards Poppy. Poppy was almost cowering away from the Victor-cat, her tail flicking and her teeth bared. The Victor-cat started pacing the floor, circling Jack and Katherine who both watched its progress, eyes transfixed. It had a very superior look on its hard face as it kept the little cat and the tailless dog in its vision.

Jack kept glancing at Poppy; he was desperate to make sure nothing was happening to her, he was not even sure if there were any physical signs when a morpher lost their mind and became wholly the animal whose shape he had assumed. Jack had no idea how long it would normally take for this process to grab hold, Victor had said a couple of hours and Jack was guessing he might have had some experience of this sort of thing. Okay, so if it normally took a couple of hours, they could expect maybe another couple of hours from the back-up discs, but Jack could not be sure of this, of course. As he was guessing, he knew he should err on the side of caution and try and come up with some sort of plan to get them out of there as soon as possible. Looking around he assessed their situation. The Victor-cat was still circling them, it looked very strong and fast but it also had the same injury both Jack and Katherine had; they all had oozing cuts on their front left legs which could slow them all down. There were also two Bangers in the room: the bland, ordinary man that Jack had not recognised, who had fetched them from the bedroom, and the one Victor had called Alfie, who also had a cut on his wrist, but his was still bandaged and would probably remain so unless he morphed. The Telling Cups room was big and bare and had floor to ceiling windows, none of which were open. From the tour Jack had been on earlier, he knew this room was on the ground floor and that outside was a large patio area leading onto a pristine lawn, none of which could be seen because it was dark outside; the darkness, Jack knew, would be an advantage if they could just get out of this room. The Victor-cat watched Jack as he looked around the room, looking for a means of escape. Although in his present form Victor could not speak, he stared at Jack with a look that said, *you are wasting your time, you cannot escape from me*, and Jack was sure he saw the big cat smile!

Time seemed to stand still as they all stood there staring at each other, although, in reality, Jack knew time was not standing still at all and that every minute they were not escaping was another minute they lost. He could feel the hopeless panic rising in him; he had no plan, he did not even have an idea for a plan. He moved closer to Poppy until they were touching. The little cat looked up at him; he wished he could reassure her that everything would be okay, but right now he did not have any confidence that it would be.

Then Jack felt rather than saw the Victor-cat stop pacing; he looked up and saw Victor standing, staring at the floor, twitching slightly. Jack watched in fascinated horror as the

Victor-cat fell to the ground and started writhing, making no sound, but thrashing and convulsing. Jack had no idea what was happening, but the two Bangers in the room looked terrified so Jack could only assume this was not normal. The Victor-cat continued to move across the floor, looking like it was having a fit, for a few more minutes. The room was completely silent, everyone in it, human and animal, staring, transfixed, until suddenly it stopped, dead still and just lay on the floor, not moving. After a few minutes Jack was just beginning to think it might be dead when the big cat moved; just slow movements at first, but eventually it got shakily to its feet, slightly wobbly the cat stood and looked around. It looked confused, a little scared even, not at all the confident cat it had been before.

It stared at Jack and Jack stared back. There was something different though, something wrong, something had changed since the Victor-cat had fallen to the floor. Jack stared at the cat; what was it, why did it look so different? Then he realised, the eyes: the cold black eyes were gone, replaced by yellowy-green eyes with cat-like pupils. *Cats' eyes* not human eyes. Weren't the eyes the only things that did not change when a morpher morphed? Weren't the eyes supposed to be the only way to tell? Jack looked at Poppy, her beautiful blue-green eyes looking at him, her beautiful blue-green *human* eyes. He looked back to the Victor-cat, but there was no trace of Victor in those eyes, no trace of human at all. Then the Banger called Alfie spoke, making Jack jump.

'Vic?' he said tentatively. 'Vic, you okay?'

The Victor-cat took no notice; it just continued to stare at Jack.

'Vic?' Alfie almost screamed the name this time.

The Victor-cat looked round at the Banger then fled towards the door; its large frame pushed until the double doors burst open and it disappeared through them. Alfie and the bland

Banger ran after the cat leaving Prince and Poppy alone in the Telling Cups room. It was all Jack needed, he looked at Poppy and then looked at the open doors and they both ran for their lives, through the double doors into the huge hallway, their paws slipping on the polished surface, slowing them slightly. The Victor-cat had obviously forced its way out of the front door as well because the heavy wood was splintered and hanging off on one hinge. Jack and Poppy easily ran through the gap into the night beyond.

It was dark outside, but the moon was bright, casting an eerie glow and thousands of stars twinkled brightly. There was light coming from the house as well, spilling through the windows, lighting the garden outside. Once through the front door, Prince and Poppy kept to the shadows, creeping along the side of the house towards the long drive. They could not see anyone or any movement. The Victor-cat and the two Bangers were nowhere to be seen. Everything was still and quiet, but Jack was not prepared to take any unnecessary chances, even though every fibre of his being wanted to run as fast as he could, he kept them as hidden as possible and this meant that the going was slow. Poppy stuck to his side, he could feel her little body trembling with fear. The cuts on both their front legs were now bleeding freely after their brief, but very fast exit from the house. Although the stitches were still holding, just, blood poured between each of them. Jack was very aware that this would not only slow them down, but it was leaving a trail that would be easy to follow; he had no time to think about that now. They reached the end of the house and could see the driveway twisting into the distance. Jack knew they would have to leave the relative safety of the shadows to get down the drive. He looked around, he could not see anyone. He looked at Poppy, then he looked towards the drive and hoped she understood. She did. They both ran as fast as they could onto the drive and followed it towards the gate. Luckily the driveway was quite shady and the further they got from the house the darker it became, so the tailless dog and the little cat were able to run without being seen. It was a long drive; Jack remembered that from his journey to Jackson Hall with the Bangers. They ran, blood flying behind them. Eventually Jack could see the gates; his heart racing, he glanced at Poppy, she was keeping up with his pace. When he looked back towards the gates though, his heart almost stopped; right in the middle of the drive, right between the two large open gates, stood the Victor-cat, pacing backwards and forwards. Prince and Poppy both skidded to a halt, gravel flying. The Victor-cat stopped pacing and looked at them, they stared back, frozen to the spot. The large cat sniffed the air and Jack wondered if he was smelling their blood. Then the Banger called Alfie stepped out of the shadows and walked towards the Victor-cat. The Victor-cat stared at Alfie, then he stared at Prince and Poppy; he took a small step towards them, sniffed again, and then took off at a run into the shadows by the side of the gate and Alfie followed him.

Prince and Poppy looked at each other and then ran through the open gates, they ran and ran until they could run no more.

They were lost. They had run for a very long time, how long Jack did not know, but it was starting to get light. They had stopped when it had started pouring with rain and they spotted an old shed on someone's allotment. They had pushed the door and to their great relief it had opened. As they rested, the quick healing process that Jack had experienced before started to get to work and before much time had passed both their cuts had stopped bleeding and the skin had fused together. The cuts were still sore, but at least the blood had stopped. Although they had managed to escape from Jackson Hall and Victor, their situation had not improved much. They were lost; they had no idea where they were. Neither of them had any idea where Jackson Hall was situated, so they had no idea where in England they were, if indeed, they were in England. Jack was very aware that they had both been animals for quite a long time, he was not sure how long, but he was sure every minute counted now. He knew that they should morph to humans, but they were both soaked through from the rain and Jack remembered Katherine telling him the Anny Mall was under cover because morphing when wet was not easy. They would have wait until they were dry. Besides, they were both stuck as animals for other reasons too: they could not morph into humans because they had no clothes and, even if they did become human, they had no money, no phone, nothing. They were hungry and thirsty and tired, and they had no idea how long they had left on the back-up discs. The only improvement that their escape had made was that they were no longer prisoners. Sitting snuggled together in the damp shed, exhausted, they both fell asleep before they had a chance to dry.

Jack awoke with a start; for a few moments he could not remember where he was. He looked blearily around and then remembered the escape from Jackson Hall and the shed they had found to shelter from the rain. How long had they been asleep? How much longer would their back-up discs last? He was still thinking like a human so the disc must still be working, he hoped and prayed that Katherine's was still okay. He shook Poppy awake; she looked up at him looking as confused as he had felt when he had just woken up. They had to morph into humans now that they were dry, even if it was only for a few minutes, and then they could morph back. Jack started morphing and, to his relief, once she realised what he was doing, Katherine morphed as well. Once they were both human, they started shivering. They found an old pair of overalls, which Jack put on, and some old potato sacks which they ripped some holes in and made a makeshift dress for Katherine.

'Thank goodness we can still morph into humans,' Jack said, 'I don't know long we were asleep, but at least the discs did their job.'

Katherine nodded, looking sad.

'Where are we, Jack?' she asked. 'Do you have any idea?'

'No,' Jack said simply. 'I was in the back of a van on the way to Jackson Hall, I couldn't see anything.'

'Me too,' said Katherine. 'I don't even know what direction we were going in, how are we going to get home? We don't know where we are and we have no money.'

'I know,' said Jack. 'I've been trying to think of something, but our situation isn't looking good. We need to look at this logically, now we have clothes, of sorts.' He looked down at the old tattered overalls. 'We could change back to animals, as long as we take the clothes with us, then we need to find a shop or hotel or something where we can become human again and ask where we are. Once we have this information at least we'll know how far from home we are.'

'Brilliant,' Katherine smiled. 'Let's go.'

'Excuse me, sir,' Jack said to the man behind the counter. The man was looking at Jack as though he had just crawled out from under a stone. It was little wonder, Jack was standing there in too-small overalls that were caked in dried mud and he had bare feet. Katherine did not look much better: the sack-dress was very frayed and smelled musty and she too had bare feet. Plus they both had angry looking scars on their left arms. Prince and Poppy had left the shed with Prince carrying the clothes in his mouth; it had felt very uncomfortable to Jack. They had then walked for at least an hour until they had found a petrol station.

Morphing into human form and putting on the clothes in the toilets, they now stood in front of the petrol station attendant.

'I'm sorry to bother you, but we seem to be lost. I wonder, could you please tell me where we are?' Jack said as politely as he could.

The man cleared his throat.

'Er, yeah, sure. You're just outside of Teignmouth,' the man said still staring.

'Thank you, sir,' Jack said. 'And where exactly is Teignmouth, please?'

'Devon,' the man replied.

'Thank you.'

They left the petrol station. Once outside they turned to each other.

'Devon,' they both said at the same time.

'At least we're still in England,' said Katherine. 'If we can find a phone, I can call Uncle Leo, reverse the charges and ask him to send us some money, then we can buy some proper clothes and get a train or something.'

Jack kissed her, for the first time since losing her in the park he felt happy and relaxed, everything was going to be okay.

Sitting on the train, holding hands, they both fell asleep. Doctor Noah had been so relieved to hear from Katherine, he had been out of his mind with worry, she assured him they were both fine and would tell him the whole story as soon as they got home. As good as his word, Dr Noah had immediately sent them some money to a local post office. They had bought warm clothes and shoes. They had not eaten for what seemed like ages so they went to a local supermarket where they bought sandwiches and cakes and cans of Coke to have on the train. Now they were on their way home. Feeling safe and relaxed, stomachs full, neither of them had been able to keep their eyes open.

Dr Noah had met them at the station several hours later; he had hugged Katherine as though he never wanted to let her go.

'Tell me what happened,' he demanded.

'Can it wait 'til we get home?' Katherine had begged, 'I desperately need a shower.'

Dr Noah had smiled at this.

'Yes, I guess it can wait a little longer,' he said. 'But then I want the whole story you understand, everything, from beginning to end, leave nothing out.'

At this he had looked at Jack, Jack was not sure what he meant but he was too tired to worry too much about it.

The car journey home had been quiet; no one had spoken.

As soon as they got back to Dr Noah's house, Katherine had gone for a shower and Jack had phoned his grandma, who, like Dr Noah had been going mad with worry. Jack assured her he was fine and would be home soon. He had no idea what he was going to tell her, but he would worry about that later.

Once he too had had a shower, they all went into the living room and sat down. There was silence for a while, then Dr Noah said, 'Right, now, tell me everything.'

17.

THE VELOXER

'I don't understand,' said Jack to Dr Noah. 'I mean, how are we still human, Kat and me?'

The three of them were still sitting in Dr Noah's living room drinking hot chocolate and eating delicious homemade cakes, courtesy of Mrs Tumble. Jack and Katherine had just finished telling Dr Noah about everything that had happened to them since they had been playing tennis; how Katherine had been taken by the Bangers, how Jack had received the text and gone to the alley, where the Bangers had taken him too, how they had been locked in the bedroom at Jackson Hall, how they had both had their interrupters stolen, how Victor Bang had morphed into the Victor-cat and how he had gone all funny and his eyes had changed, (Dr Noah had smiled at this) and how they had escaped, everything right up the point where Katherine had phoned Dr Noah.

Dr Noah had looked sternly at Jack when they had explained about morphing into humans in the shed and having to find clothes, but Katherine had exclaimed loudly that it was when she had been in least danger and had he not listened to what Victor had done to them, that Dr Noah had relaxed.

After a few moments of silence and a reassuring smile from

Dr Noah, Jack had felt it was okay to continue.

'Why didn't we lose our minds? We stayed as animals for ages, how long do those back-up discs last?' Jack asked.

Dr Noah stood up and started pacing the room; he stopped and looked at Jack.

'The thing is, Jackson, they were not back-up discs that I inserted in yours and Katherine's right arms – they were interrupters. Not the normal interrupter like you had before, but an extremely powerful new interrupter. This new interrupter, known as a *deallus*, is very powerful, much smaller than a normal interrupter, and can be inserted in either the left or right arm and, as you know, is almost undetectable to the eye – unlike the interrupter. I've been working on it for a while now.'

Jack looked at Katherine; she shrugged as if to say it was news to her, too.

'So why didn't you tell us that before?' Jack asked. 'Why did you tell us they were back-up discs designed to last for a while until we could morph back?'

'Because, I knew if your interrupters were stolen, the best thing for you would be to get to me as soon as possible. If you had known you had a deallus, and knew what it could do, you would not have felt any urgency in getting to see me. Luckily the doctor who removed your interrupters actually did quite a good job; your wounds are clean and neat, but they might not have been...' Dr Noah trailed off.

'So why did we need the interrupters as well? Why didn't you remove them?' Jack asked.

'Because I knew the Bangers would come after you again, I knew they wanted your disc.' Dr Noah was silent for a few moments then he added, 'I'm sorry, Jackson, I took a gamble with you, luckily it paid off.'

'What gamble?' asked Katherine, sounding slightly annoyed.

Dr Noah sat down opposite Jack.

'You must understand, I know the Bangers and Victor; I know how they think, how they operate. I knew they would try again for your interrupter Jackson. I knew Victor would want it, that he would stop at nothing to get it.'

'So is it true about my dad then?' Jack asked simply.

Dr Noah did not try to pretend he did not know what Jack was talking about.

'You mean about Victor's brother Charles being your father and you having his heart? Yes, I'm sorry, I should have told you.' Dr Noah had the grace to look down as he said this.

'Yes you should've,' Jack said, though he did not sound angry, just sad.

'Would you have told me if I hadn't found out?' he asked, looking the doctor straight in the eyes.

'I don't know, maybe, one day. Anyway, when the Bangers attacked you last time I knew they would try again, so I swapped your interrupter for a veloxer.'

'A what?' Jack asked.

'A veloxer,' said Dr Noah.

'What's a veloxer?'

'Well, it's almost the opposite of an interrupter; if an interrupter keeps your mind human when you take on the form of an animal, then a veloxer forces your mind to become like the animal and stop being human, it sort of speeds up the natural process. When Victor had that disc inserted into his arm, without the added protection of the deallus, the veloxer was just waiting for him to morph; the moment he did, it got to work. When Victor dropped to the floor that was the veloxer starting the process, by the time he stood up it was all over. You say his eyes changed?'

Katherine and Jack both nodded.

'Well that's proof. The eyes never change, never, not unless the mind has gone, then they change, they become that of the animal, no longer human, that's the sign.'

There was silence. No one spoke for a while.

'Are you saying Victor's gone for good? That he can never be human again?' Jack asked.

'Yes, that's exactly what I'm saying. He can never morph back, his mind can no longer cope with human thoughts, he has the mind of a cat and, as far as he is concerned, he always has, he will not remember being human at all.'

Silence again. Then Katherine said, 'You shouldn't have used Jack like that, you should've told him.'

'I'm sorry,' Dr Noah said. 'I thought I was acting for the best. I thought if I told you, Jackson you might give the game away. I am sorry,' he said again.

Jack shrugged, looking at his lap.

'And something else,' Dr Noah said, looking at Jack. Jack looked up.

'Jackson, I want to thank you.'

Jack looked quizzically at Dr Noah.

'I want to thank you for going after Katherine; that took a lot of bravery. I want to thank you for looking after her, for caring about her.'

'S'nothing,' said Jack. 'I love her.'

Dr Noah smiled and Katherine burst into tears.

A few hours later, having had his wound re-dressed by Dr Noah and having eaten so many cakes he felt sick, Jack was at home trying to explain to his grandma where he had been. Obviously he could not tell her the truth, so he had made up a story about Katherine being taken ill and Dr Noah not being around and he, Jack, having to get her to a hospital and how he had forgotten his phone. His grandma had found his phone on his bed so she believed that bit, but the look on her face told him she did not believe a word of the rest of it. She did, however, accept the story.

'Jack, sweetie,' she said once he was done telling his story. 'I need to talk to you.'

She looked strained and Jack was suddenly concerned about her. He had not spent a lot of time with her lately, too busy working at the sanctuary or being with Katherine to have noticed how old she was looking or how frail she seemed to have become. He felt guilty.

'Gran,' he started. 'I'm sorry I haven't been around much lately, I'll...'

But she cut him off saying.

'Oh, Jack, don't be silly, you have your own life, I don't begrudge you that. You're young, you have stuff to do.' she smiled, 'that's sort of what I want to talk to you about. This house, it's, well I'm not happy here anymore, Jack. Ever since your granddad died I've felt this place is just too big for the two of us. Do you remember my friend, Sue?'

Jack looked puzzled.

'Sue?' Pam repeated. 'You know, I stayed with her after the funeral? Down by the sea?'

'Oh yeah,' Jack remembered.

'Well, we've been talking and...' she seemed to be searching for the words.

'You want to go and live with her?' Jack offered.

Pam smiled.

'Yes.' She sounded relieved, 'Well, we want to buy somewhere together. You can come with me,' she added quickly, 'Sue and I have discussed that, you're very welcome.' But she seemed to know from the look on his face what he would say to that.

'Thanks, Gran.' He moved closer and pulled her into a hug. 'I think it's a great idea for you to go and live with your friend, but I think I'll stay here, you know, with Kat.'

She pulled away and smiled up at him.

'I thought you'd say that.' She looked a bit sad, but then she added, 'From the sale of this house I can buy the place with Sue; we've already found somewhere we like, and still have enough to buy you a flat here.'

Jack started to say that she did not have to do that, but Pam cut him off again, insisting she wanted to and it was what his granddad would have wanted.

Lying in bed later that evening, Jack stared at the ceiling. It all seemed so final, his gran moving away; he knew it was for the best, but it felt like it was the end of something, the end of his childhood.

The following day Jack found several missed calls from Dennis on his phone, he rang Dennis' number and almost jumped when, as soon as Dennis answered, he shouted down the phone at Jack.

'I did it, I passed!'

'Passed what?' asked Jack, holding the phone away from his ear, not understanding what Dennis meant.

'My driving test, mate. I passed.' Dennis sounded ecstatic. Then he added, 'Where have you been, mate, I've been ringing and ringing.'

Jack mumbled a shorter version of the same cobbled story to Dennis that he had told his gran, and as Dennis was only half listening anyway, he did not question it.

'I've even got a car,' Dennis almost shouted again as soon as Jack stopped talking.

So they chatted happily for a few minutes before Jack hung up, promising to go out for a spin in the new car the next day.

Over the next few weeks Jack's life settled back to some sort of normal. He told the same story to Nora and Mr Fielding to explain why he had been away for a few days and missed work; they, like Dennis, accepted it without question, they were just glad to have their best worker back.

One thing that did not get back to normal, however, were Jack's dreams. Since leaving Jackson Hall, he had not had the running dream at all. He was not sorry about this, but he was intrigued. The dream that had controlled most of his sleeping hours had vanished completely. Was it because he now understood what and who he was, had the dream been trying to tell him about the morphing? Or had it been trying to warn him about what was going to happen to Katherine and therefore was no longer relevant? He did not know and probably never would. All he did know was that every night he was happy to fall into dreamless sleep and keep the running for his waking hours.

'It's perfect!' Katherine exclaimed for the umpteenth time. 'Just perfect!'

They were in the new flat Pam had bought for Jack. It was a first floor maisonette in an old converted house with two bedrooms, a living room, kitchen, bathroom and a small garden. It was situated in Tenbridge, not too far from the sanctuary where Jack worked. Jack had moved in that very day. He had some furniture; Pam had not needed all the stuff from the house, so he at least had a bed and something to sit on, even if it was not what he would have chosen for himself.

Pam had moved into her new house with Sue the week before and Jack had been staying at Dr Noah's house until the flat was ready.

Now they were here, moving all Jack's things in, unpacking boxes and suitcases and trying to put things away in cupboards and drawers. Jack was putting stuff away in the kitchen and Katherine was in one of the bedrooms when Jack heard her call.

'Jack, Jack, come here.'

He went into the bedroom and found Katherine holding the old, black leather box with the word *Moraid* written in gold on the lid.

'What is this?' she asked.

'Oh that!' Jack exclaimed taking the box from her and looking at it. 'I'd forgotten all about that. Do you remember I told you, that's the thing that Ski guy brought round to me? It's a cuff thing.'

He handed the box back to her and said, 'Open it, have a look.'

Katherine looked at Jack and then opened the box and found the silvery metal bangle-thing that Jack had told her about at the Anny Mall when they had seen others like it. Katherine pulled the cuff out of the dark red velvet lining and twisted it in her fingers, looking at it from every angle, thinking.

'Jack, the initials inside this cuff, *CJ*, who's that? You don't think that was your dad, do you? *Charles Jackson*?'

Jack looked closer at the cuff and the initials.

'S'pose it must be,' he said. 'Who else could it be?'

As they stood there, staring at it, Katherine tipped the box slightly and something fell out on to the floor. She picked it up; it was the thimble thing that had come with the cuff.

'Jack!' she exclaimed. 'Look at this.'

It was silver in colour, engraved with tiny moons and stars and set with coloured stones.

'Jack, don't you recognise this? This is the little cup; this is the smallest of the Telling Cups, Jack! You had it all the time.'

Jack looked at it; so it was, the thing he had assumed was a thimble was the very valuable cup that Victor had been so keen to find, the cup that was missing and which the other Telling Cups would not work without. He took it from Katherine and studied the engraving and the stones. If the cuff really had belonged to his father, then Victor had been right, Charles had had the little cup. Suddenly everything was falling into place.

'That bird,' Jack almost shouted. 'The one that was in my bedroom, the one who wrecked everything, it must have been searching for this. You know I told you, the bird with the funny eyes.'

He thought for a moment; those eyes, one dark brown and one half dark brown and half green, they were very distinct. Where had he seen those eyes? And then it came to him.

'That woman!' again he almost shouted.

'What woman?' Katherine asked.

'The one with Victor – Demetria, was it? She had funny eyes and she asked Victor about the missing Telling Cup, what if she was the bird?'

Silence had followed as they both thought about things for a while and then Katherine put the cuff and the cup back in the leather box. She handed the box to Jack.

'You better keep this safe,' she said, 'that cup is priceless.'

A few hours later, they finished unpacking and fell exhausted on to the settee; it had been a long and tiring day. Jack phoned for pizza and they watched the TV while they waited for it to be delivered.

'Kat,' Jack said; he could hear the nerves in his own voice. 'Kat, there's something I want to ask you, something I've wanted to ask you for a while.'

'What?' she looked away from the TV and at him.

Jack took a deep breath and exhaled through his mouth.

'Kat,' he repeated. 'You know how I feel about you, don't you? You know I love you and want to be with you?'

She nodded.

'And I love you,' she said, 'and I want to be with you, too.'

'Then how would you feel about moving in with me? Here?' he added. He said all this very quickly. Red-faced, Jack fumbled with something in his pocket, tugging it, it eventually became free and Katherine could see it was small red leather box, he handed it to her. She opened the box very carefully, nestled in the deep red silk lining was a gold ring, a plain gold band with a loop on the top that held a gold heart charm set with a greenish-blue stone.

'Reminded me of your eyes,' Jack mumbled looking at the floor, 'the stone, you know.' He looked up at her.

There was silence for a few moments as Katherine slipped the ring onto her finger, then her beautiful face split into a huge smile. She turned around to face him properly and threw her arms around his neck and kissed him. Then she broke away and looked deep into his eyes.

'I'd love to, yes!' she said, and then she added. 'Meow.'